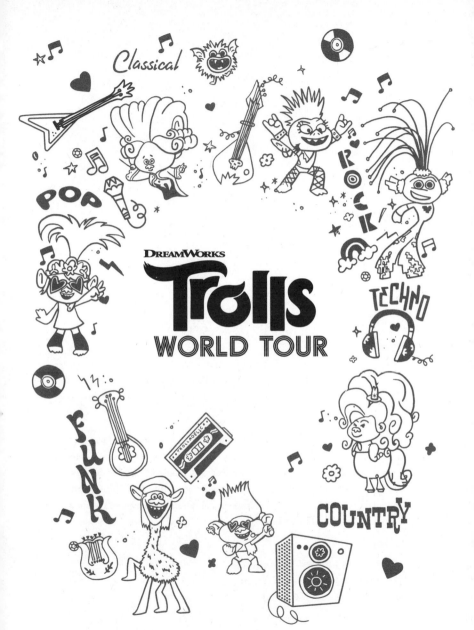

rhcbooks.com

ISBN 978-0-593-12290-7 (hardcover)
ISBN 978-0-593-12291-4 (paperback)
ISBN 978-0-593-12292-1 (ebook)

Printed in the United States of America

10 9 8 7 6 5 4 3 2 1

DREAMWORKS

Trolls
WORLD TOUR

The Deluxe Junior Novelization

Adapted by David Lewman

Random House 🏠 New York

CHAPTER ONE

Once upon a time, two Trolls named Poppy and Branch saved the world. Poppy became queen, Branch found his true colors, and they became best friends. Hooray!

What Poppy and Branch didn't know was that their world was a lot bigger than they thought. Like, a lot bigger.

Imagine a scene like this:

Deep, deep in the dark ocean depths lies the watery kingdom of the Techno Trolls. The inky darkness pulses with neon lights as the Trolls' beautiful, shimmering mermaid tails wave in unison. They dance to the pounding, throbbing beats of

their Techno music. THOOMPA! THOOMPA! THOOMPA! THOOMPA! *It's like every night is the best night ever!*

It is at one of these nightly dance parties that our story begins . . . to go wrong. So wrong. Just keep reading. You'll see. . . .

King Trollex was playing a thumping Techno song from his royal DJ booth. *"One more time!"* he sang to his fellow Techno Trolls, who were overjoyed by the sound of the beats. He swam around the booth, swishing his plaid fins, his glowing green hair waving in the water.

A whole family of Techno Trolls danced along to the music—even their baby! He felt the music from the tip of his tail to the top of his single strand of hair. His tiny heart was visible through his translucent body, lighting up in time to the rhythm of the tune. And he wasn't the only one—all the Techno Trolls' hearts were beating together as one.

Putting on his headphones, King Trollex called out, "What's up, my Techno Trolls?" He pumped his rainbow-striped arms over his head.

The crowd cheered. They loved their undersea

kingdom, their king, and their driving techno beats.

"Tonight is about family, love, and music," King Trollex continued. "Come on . . . let me see you jump! One, two, three, four!"

The Techno Trolls jumped in groups, sending a wave pattern circling around the town center.

"Get ready for the drop!" the king shouted. He swam around his booth, using the power of his tail to glide through the water. As he swam, the crowd's anticipation for the musical drop—when the beat changed—grew and grew.

King Trollex paused in front of his control panel and looked down at the button for the drop. "Are you ready?" he asked the cheering crowd, which throbbed up and down like musical sound waves.

King Trollex smiled. "Wait for it . . . ," he said to himself as the crowd grew wilder. "Wait for it . . . wait for it . . . wait for it . . . ." He swam through the dancers, who were practically losing their minds.

King Trollex let the tension build.

"Just do it already!" a Techno Troll shouted.

Finally, King Trollex said, "One more time!"

BOOM. He slammed his fist on the beat-drop button, and the beat finally dropped! The crowd of dancing Techno Trolls went positively wild, loving it! They jumped, swayed, and shimmied to the beat of the music.

In the distance, a large dark creature swam toward the bright lights of the dance party.

King Trollex noticed the looming figure approaching. He squinted, trying to make out what it was. It didn't look friendly.

The king pressed another button, and the techno music faded out. All the Trolls looked up, disappointed. "Don't worry, everybody," King Trollex reassured them. "We'll get back to the party in a minute. Let me just take care of this real quick."

He turned to face the creature as it cruised closer. It was black and covered in spikes, with a single big red eye. A sign on its side read ROCK TOUR. Though King Trollex didn't know it, this fishy beast served as a tour bus. It looked as though it had been made from scraps of denim and black leather, held together with heavy zippers. It was *not* a friendly look. Half a dozen similar creatures swam up next to it and looked just as menacing.

The lead creature's mouth slowly unzipped with a horrible grinding metal noise to reveal its pilot.

She was dressed in black leather and denim with a Mohawk haircut standing straight up from her head. She wore two earrings in her right ear, one earring in her left ear, and a black leather band with metal studs on her wrist.

"Hey, man!" Her eyes glowed red. "There he is! King Trollex of the Techno Trolls, right?"

Trollex looked up at her, surprised that this stranger knew his name. What did she want? "That's right," he said. "Who's asking?"

"Queen Barb," the pilot answered. "Of the Rocker Trolls. Didn't you get my invitation? I could have sworn I sent you one."

King Trollex didn't remember any invitation. He turned to his fellow Techno Trolls. "Uh, did anybody see an invitation?" he asked.

"Nope," a Techno Troll at the back of the crowd called out. "No invitation."

King shrugged. "Mail's a pretty low priority around here."

"Okay, cool-cool-cool," Queen Barb said. "Well, it just would've explained that I'm throwing the biggest party the world has ever seen, and . . . I'm going to need your string, bro."

The Techno Trolls frowned. Their string? They couldn't give away their string. It was too important! They needed it to make their music!

King Trollex had no intention of giving away the Techno Trolls' string.

"No way," he told Queen Barb. "If we lose our string, we lose our music."

Queen Barb smiled. But no one would mistake it for a friendly smile. It was pretty scary, actually.

"Oh, you mean your bleeps and bloops?" Queen Barb sneered. She sarcastically imitated the sound of the electronic Techno music. *"Beep-beep-beep bwoop."* Still smiling her nasty smile, she shook her head. "Yeah, that's not music. Do you wanna hear some real music?" She called out, "ROCKERS!"

More glowing red eyes appeared around the Techno Trolls—Queen Barb's rockers. King Trollex looked frightened, and so did the beat-drop button and the other Techno Trolls. Queen Barb's creatures unzipped their mouths, revealing the Rocker Trolls within.

KA-WHAM! With a thunderous opening chord, the rockers started to play blaring rock music, blasting it at peak volume. Queen Barb's drummer,

Riff, sat behind a huge set of drums. He pounded out a flashy drumroll, slammed his head into a tom-tom, and hit the cymbals with both sticks. *CRASH!* An underwater shock wave rolled through, driving back King Trollex and the rest of the Techno Trolls.

It didn't stop there. *KA-WHEEM! KA-WHOM! KA-WHAMMY!* The Rocker Trolls unleashed the full power of their instruments on the poor Techno Trolls.

"Okay, okay, enough! Stop!" King Trollex cried, covering his ears. "You're harshing the vibe we worked very hard to build."

Queen Barb grinned an evil grin. "But by the end of my world tour, bro, we're all going to have the same vibe. We're all going to be One Nation of Trolls, Under Rock!"

She grabbed an electric guitar and thrashed out a massive chord, sending off a huge rock shock wave that destroyed the coral reef under the DJ booth. *WHA-RAAMMMMM!*

"WHO'S READY TO ROCK?" Queen Barb screeched.

CHAPTER TWO

The next morning in the faraway land of the Pop Trolls, Queen Poppy woke up in her fuzzy pod home, which hung from the branch of a huge, thick tree. She jumped out of bed, eager to start a new day. First, she hopped into her glitter shower. (There's nothing like a stream of shiny glitter to make you feel sparkling fresh!) Then she brushed her teeth with a lollipop (a method that works just fine for Trolls, but isn't recommended for human beings). As she brushed, each tooth temporarily turned a different color!

After Poppy's shower, she sang a song about how happy she was to be queen, and how Trolls loved having fun. Glowbugs flew over with her blue dress. They dropped it over her head, and she wriggled into it. She danced over to a mirror and fixed her hair as the Glowbugs gently placed her crown on her head. Proud of their accomplishment, the Glowbugs high-fived. *SMACK!*

Poppy was still singing as she flung open the doors of her pod. Outside in the bright sunlight, all the other Trolls in the village were gathered in the village square, singing and dancing. Queen Poppy quickly joined their dance, spinning and kicking as they sang a happy pop tune about Troll life: HAVING FUN!

Actually, not *all* the Trolls were there. Branch was still in his heavily fortified underground bunker. In his hand he held a framed picture covered with a sign that read NOTHING IMPORTANT. He lifted the sign and stared at a picture of himself with Poppy. He sighed. He wanted to tell the queen how he felt about her—he liked her *a lot*—but could never seem to summon the courage. Maybe the morning dance would help psych him up! He decided to go up and dive in!

Outside, he jumped onto a flower. *SPROING!* The flower vaulted him high into the air. With his hair, he caught a zip line and slid into the village square, dropping right next to Poppy. She smiled at Branch, and he fell in with the morning's song and dance.

But to him, Troll life wasn't just about fun and games. Poppy was now their queen, with official duties, and Branch was going to do everything he could to help her perform them as smoothly and easily as possible. This took planning.

"All right, Queen Poppy," Branch said, trying to get down to business even though the song was still going on. Poppy was only halfway paying attention to him. "I've prepared an agenda for the day." He propped up a board with a list displayed in his clear, bold handwriting.

"I hope it says 'singing, dancing, and hugging,'" Poppy said.

"Uh, isn't that what we do *every* day?" Branch asked.

"Yeah!" Poppy said, holding up a pair of colorful skates. "Good times!"

She thought about a happy day earlier in the week, when she and her friends had skated around the village singing a pop tune about good times.

She was still lost in the memory when she heard a familiar voice yell, "Poppy, come quick! It's an EMERGENCY!"

She and Branch ran over to a nearby clearing and found the village's most glittery Troll, Guy Diamond, sitting on a purple mushroom. He looked scared.

"What's wrong?" Poppy asked, concerned.

"I'm having a . . . BABY!" Guy cried.

Satin and Chenille, the twin Trolls who were connected by their rainbow hair, urgently knitted outfits for the new baby. "We're on jumpsuit duty!" they said in unison.

Cooper, the village's most unusual Troll, with his four legs and green felt hat, was excited. "I get to be a role model!"

"I don't *want* to be a *big* sister," tiny Smidge pouted.

POP! A little egg burst out of Guy's silver hair! It cracked open in midair, and a tiny glitter Troll came out! Silver with a green nose, the little one was sucking his thumb.

"Awwwww," everyone gushed when they saw the cute new Troll.

"What should I name him?" Guy Diamond asked, thrilled.

"Hmm," Poppy said, thinking. "How about . . . Tiny Diamond?"

Tiny Diamond jumped to his feet and put on big square sunglasses with yellow lenses and thick black frames. He surprised the Trolls by delivering an expert rap in a deep voice. They loved the little Troll's large personality—and the big finish to his song ending in an explosion of glitter was better than fireworks!

To celebrate the arrival of Tiny Diamond, all the Trolls sang and danced, bouncing upside down on their hair, building to a grand finale. Another fun, super-sunshiny day had begun.

CHAPTER THREE

As the Trolls started off for the day's activities, Poppy complimented them on their fine performances in their morning song and dance. "Hey, that was some fancy footwork, Cooper!" she called out.

"Some people just got it," Cooper said, grinning and doing a funky little move.

"Biggie! Mr. Dinkles!" she said to the big blue Troll and his beloved pet worm. "You two were on fire." In fact, Mr. Dinkles still had a few flames flickering on him.

"Yeah," Biggie said apologetically. "Sorry about that, Queen Poppy." He quickly put out Mr. Dinkles's flames and made sure he was okay.

"Mew," Mr. Dinkles said, a little smoke rising from his round mouth. He was fine.

Poppy pointed to another Troll, Legsly. She wore an ankle bracelet on one of her very stretchy legs. "I'm diggin' that new anklet, Legsly!"

"Thanks, Poppy!" Legsly called back. "Kisses and doughnuts and sprinkles!" She blew kisses and ran off to join her friends, her anklet jingling as she went. *JINGLE-JANGLE!*

"What a Troll," Branch said, amazed once again by Legsly's exceptional sweetness.

Guy Diamond walked by with Tiny Diamond perched on his shoulder, proudly showing off his new son to everyone in the village.

"Tiny Diamond!" Poppy called to the new arrival. "Welcome to the family, little buddy!"

"Thanks, Aunt Poppy!" Tiny Diamond said in his deep voice. He pointed to Guy Diamond. "And thanks to this silver-haired daddy of mine for bringing me into this world."

"I never knew my heart could be so full," Guy Diamond said joyfully in his signature auto-tuned voice.

As they walked off, Tiny Diamond threw a peace

sign from his perch on his father's glittery shoulder. "Peace and love!" he called. "Bless up. Tiny and Daddy out."

"Okay, bye!" Poppy called after them, waving.

The Trolls went their separate ways, leaving Poppy and Branch alone. Branch realized this was a good opportunity to tell Poppy just how he felt about her. He took a deep breath, squared his shoulders, and walked up to her.

"Hey, um, Poppy?" he said, trying to sound casual and not at all nervous. "There's something I was hoping to ask you. I mean, I guess it's something I want to *tell* you. . . ."

They strolled over to a garden full of flowers. Poppy nuzzled a fuzzy, buglike creature, then picked up a can full of glitter water and began to water the flowers. "Uh-huh . . . ," she said as she tended to the plants.

"But listen," Branch continued a bit awkwardly. "You could feel free to respond to what I tell you with an answer if you wanted." *Ugh, this is NOT going the way I planned,* Branch thought. *It is NOT going smoothly at all.*

"Sure, what's up?" Poppy said pleasantly.

"What's up is . . . ," Branch said hesitantly, "I . . . I . . . I . . . wanted to tell you that . . ."

He trailed off. He just couldn't tell her. What if she rejected him? What if she was disgusted? What if she laughed at him? Branch didn't think he could handle that. Not at all. The risk of revealing exactly how he felt was just too great. He couldn't do it.

Poppy looked at Branch expectantly.

He sighed. He couldn't say what he wanted to say, but now he had to say *something*. So he just went with a general compliment. "You're crushing it at this queen thing."

Poppy smiled. "Aw, Branch. Thank you! Being a good queen is the most important thing in the world to me. Other than being your friend."

Branch heard the word "friend" echoing in his mind. "Friend . . . friend . . . friend . . ."

He shook his head and snapped out of his romantic funk, but still just stood there awkwardly. Poppy noticed.

"Uhhh, five it up?" she said, raising her hand to high-five her friend. Branch tried to slap her hand, but missed completely. *WHIFF!*

Poppy looked puzzled. Usually her high fives

were great! "Huh," she said. "Could've been better. Let's try that again."

She held her hand up. Branch swiped his hand at it. *WHIFF!*

"Okay, one more," Poppy said, certain the first two misses had just been flukes.

This time when Branch tried to high-five Poppy, their pinky fingers just barely brushed each other. Technically, it wasn't a miss. But it also wasn't much of a high five without the satisfying *SMACK.*

"Huh," Poppy said, genuinely confused. "For some reason we can't seem to make a good connection."

Branch grabbed his chest and groaned. If he and Poppy couldn't even make a good high five connection, how could he hope they'd ever be more than friends?

Then he had a comforting thought. Maybe it wasn't him. Maybe Poppy was just having an off day, and she wasn't able to make a good high five with anyone. For that matter, maybe everyone in Trolls Village was having a bad high five day. It could be something in the weather, or the air, or—

SMACK! Fuzzbert, the hairiest Troll in the village, ran by and stuck a giant hand out of his long green hair. Poppy gave it a resounding high five.

"Ah, yes, Fuzzbert!" she cried happily. "Now, *that's* a good connection!"

Branch grabbed his chest and groaned again.

But his groan was drowned out by a loud scream! "AAAHHHHHHH!"

CHAPTER FOUR

Poppy and Branch looked at each other. What was *that*?

Poppy dropped her watering can and ran toward the scream with Branch right behind her. They didn't have to run far before they spotted Biggie, screaming and running around a clearing. A fuzzy creature resembling a bat was flying around Biggie's head. It had black, leathery wings, white fuzz around its head, big red eyes, long teeth, and two purple feet. The fuzzy thing was carrying an envelope in its mouth.

"Biggie?" Poppy said.

"Help!" Biggie cried. "I'm being harangued by a monster!"

Biggie frantically pushed through a crowd of Trolls, but the critter kept flapping around his head. Finally Biggie gave up and lay down on the ground, curling into a ball. The scraggly-looking bat kept smacking Biggie in the face over and over. *WHAP! WHAP! WHAP!*

"Someone stop it!" Biggie pleaded.

Poppy ran up to Biggie and used her hair to snatch the bat-thing out of the air. "Gotcha!" she said triumphantly. Then she realized it was now in her hair! "Ahhh! It's in my hair! It's in my hair! Get it out, get it out, get it out!"

With a fierce battle cry, Branch dove at Poppy. "YAAAAAAH!"

He tackled Poppy and the creature to the ground. Then he yanked the bat-thing from Poppy's hair and placed it on the ground on its back. He rubbed its fuzzy belly to calm it down.

"Shhh, shhh, shhh, shhh, shhhhhh," Branch soothed. "There you go. There you go. Calm down. Who's a good boy? You're a good boy."

The bat-critter stopped flapping its wings. Then it closed its big red eyes and started to purr. *"Rrrrr-trrrrr-rrrrrr . . ."*

Once Branch had gotten the creature calmed down, the other Trolls cautiously approached to get a closer look.

"What *is* that thing?" Legsly asked.

"It's creepy!" Cooper said, shuddering.

"It's scary!" Satin and Chenille said at the same time.

"And . . . naaaaaaasty," Guy Diamond said in his electronic .

"Hold me, Daddy," Tiny Diamond said in his deep voice, scared of the bizarre animal.

Poppy looked over at the rolled-up tube the bat-thing had dropped when Branch had tackled them. She walked over and picked it up.

" 'To Queen Poppy'?" she read, surprised to see her own name on the mysterious piece of mail. Then she realized what it must be—an invitation!

"Oh, don't worry, everyone!" she reassured her fellow Trolls. "It looks like it's just an invitation."

"Ohhhhh," Cooper said. "That's a relief."

"Whew." Satin and Chenille sighed at the same time.

"What's an invitation, Daddy?" Tiny Diamond asked.

As Guy Diamond lovingly explained what an invitation was, Poppy unrolled the message and read it out loud. " 'Barb, Queen of Rock, announces her **One Nation of Trolls Under Rock World Tour.** Bring your string to the biggest party the world has ever seen.' " Poppy looked up, confused. "Queen of Rock? What does that mean?"

"And why does she need our string?" Cooper asked.

"Maybe she wants to tie up a lot of presents to give away at her party," Biggie suggested.

Smidge liked Biggie's idea. "Ooooh, presents!"

They were all starting to feel much better about the fuzzy little bat and the message it had brought to them. But just as they were starting to get excited about a big party with presents, King Peppy hurried in, walking with the help of his green cane. He was clearly upset. He snatched the invitation out of his daughter's hands.

"It's nothing!" he squeaked. "It means nothing at all! It's just junk mail! You don't need to worry about it. I mean, quit looking at it! Everyone, forget what you saw!" He started chomping on the invitation, eating it!

Branch let out another fierce battle cry. "YAAAAHHHH!" He ran and tackled King Peppy to the ground and began rubbing his eyeballs to soothe him. "Shhh, shhh, shhh, shhh, shhhhh," he soothed. "There ya go. There ya go. Calm down. Calm down. . . ."

Soon King Peppy was purring, too. "Okay, I'm calm," he said after a moment. "I'm calm."

Poppy knelt beside her father and touched his shoulder gently. "Dad, what's going on?" she asked.

He paused, thinking about what to say. He didn't wanted to tell his daughter the secret he'd been keeping for so long. He wanted the problem to just go away. He sighed. Now he knew it wasn't going to be that easy.

"Well, I have long feared this day would come," King Peppy admitted. "I was hoping to protect you from this, Poppy."

Poppy looked confused, and maybe just a little bit annoyed. "Protect me?" she asked. "I'm not a little kid anymore, Dad. I'm the *queen* now."

"You're right," King Peppy said, nodding slowly. "The truth is . . . we are not alone in this world."

Mr. Dinkles made a spooky sound to accompany

King Peppy's explanation. Biggie stuck a finger in his pet worm's round mouth.

"Shhh!" Biggie said to his little friend.

"There are other kinds of Trolls," King Peppy told them. The Trolls around him were silent for a moment, taking this in. Other Trolls? What did King Peppy mean?

"Wow, really?" Poppy said enthusiastically. "Dad, that's great! The more Trolls, the merrier!"

The other Trolls nodded and smiled. Queen Poppy was right. More Trolls just meant bigger parties!

"You don't understand," King Peppy said, shaking his head. "These other Trolls aren't like us. They're . . . different."

"Different how?" Poppy asked. "Different like Legsly?"

"I love being me!" Legsly said, stretching her long legs until she stood at her full height, towering over the other Trolls, even Biggie.

"Or Fuzzbert, or Smidge, or Chris?" Poppy asked, pointing to them one by one. Fuzzbert was hairy, Smidge was tiny, and Chris looked like four Trolls on each other's shoulders stacked into one.

"Yeah, different like me?" Chris asked in his quadruple voice.

"No," King Peppy said seriously. "Not different like that."

"Then how?" Poppy asked.

CHAPTER FIVE

King Peppy paced as he answered Poppy's question. "These other Trolls are different from us in ways you can't even imagine. You see, we love music with a hummable hook. With an upbeat melody. With a catchy rhythm that makes you want to snap your fingers, tap your toes, and wiggle your butt. Right?"

"Right," the other Trolls said, nodding. That was exactly the kind of music they all loved. They sang and played it every day.

"That's pop music," King Peppy explained. "That's our music. That's what makes us Pop Trolls."

The Trolls looked surprised. They'd always just

called themselves Trolls. They'd never heard of Pop Trolls. It was strange to think that they were something they hadn't even known existed!

"But these other Trolls," King Peppy continued. "They sing different. They dance different."

The strangeness of this idea scared the Trolls. They started to panic, running around and crying, "NOOOOO!"

"STOP!" King Peppy commanded. Everyone froze. The king turned to his daughter. "How about we break down to a smaller group? I need to show you something."

King Peppy led Poppy, Branch, Biggie, Mr. Dinkles, Cooper, Smidge, Guy Diamond, Tiny Diamond, Satin, and Chenille to a beautiful grotto filled with green vines and shimmering waterfalls. In the center of the grotto was a stone pillar with an ancient scroll lying on it.

"It's a story as old as time," King Peppy said as he opened the scroll. The Trolls gathered around to look at the beautiful illustrations.

"In the beginning," King Peppy said, "there was

silence." He showed them drawings of six Trolls. "Our world was without song or dance."

In one illustration, a felt scrapbook Troll was saying, "Boring!"

King Peppy unrolled the scroll further. "Until one day, someone made a sound."

In the next drawing, a Troll was plucking a hair from the head of the Troll next to him. Above that Troll, the word "TWANG!" appeared. The other Trolls in the picture clapped and cheered.

"Our ancestors were so inspired by the sound," King Peppy went on, "that they took six strings"— he indicated an illustration of a Troll hand plucking one hair from each of the six different Trolls' heads— "and those six strings had the power to control all music!" King Peppy was clearly still excited by the old tale. "The strings could play *anything*! Techno, Funk, Classical, Country Western, Rock, and Pop. And every kind of music in between. There was something for everyone, and it was one big party."

The next picture showed Trolls dancing while a musical instrument with six strings attached to it was passed from player to player. One dancing Troll made of felt cried, "YAY!"

"But little by little," King Peppy said, "Trolls became intolerant of each other's music. They fought over the musical instrument, arguing about which kind of music they wanted to hear. And so the leaders of the Trolls held a meeting."

He unrolled more of the scroll, and everyone saw a drawing of Trolls meeting around a large table. "The Trolls elders realized there was but one solution," King Peppy said. "Each tribe would take a string and go their separate way."

The king turned the scroll's handles until he reached the end. A map showed where the six different Trolls tribes lived. "Those six tribes have lived in isolation ever since," he concluded. "Techno, Country Western, Rock, Classical, Funk, and us . . . the Pop Trolls."

He closed the scroll. The Trolls stared at each other, amazed by this information about who they were and where they'd come from.

"Now Barb's announcement makes sense," Poppy said, smiling. "She wants to reunite the strings so the Trolls world can be one big party again."

Branch was doubtful. "That's all you heard?" he

said to her. "One big party?"

"Yeah, it's when all of the Trolls lived in harmony," she said. "And what's more important than living in harmony?"

"Well, I heard fighting," Branch said. "The strings together leads to fighting."

King Peppy nodded. "Exactly, Branch. That's why we need to keep our string safe."

CHAPTER SIX

"Where *is* our string?" Poppy asked.

King Peppy turned a hidden dial. The waterfall behind him parted, revealing a musical instrument with one glowing pink string on it. "Behold the pop music string!" the king said. He plucked the string. It made a beautiful sound, sending a shimmering heart into the air.

"Ooooooooooo," everyone cooed, impressed.

"Whoa," Poppy said. "It's beautiful." She couldn't take her eyes off the colorful string.

"And powerful," King Peppy added. "Which is why we can't let it fall into the wrong hands."

Branch, with a determined look on his face, said,

"And we won't. Not on my watch. What we need is a plan." Branch was a BIG fan of planning ahead.

"Don't worry," King Peppy told him. "I've been preparing for this day for years."

"Okay," Branch said. "So what do we do?"

King Peppy gulped loudly. "WE RUN!" Then he took off fast as his stumpy legs could carry him.

Poppy looked confused. "Run?"

"*And* hide," King Peppy yelled over his shoulder. He had already covered more ground than anyone thought was possible for the old king.

"On it," Branch said. Already in full camouflage gear, he smeared dark lines under his eyes and started to run off with King Peppy.

"But we don't even know what we're running and hiding from," Poppy pointed out. Her father and Branch stopped in their tracks and turned back.

"We're hiding from Barb and all the other different Trolls," King Peppy explained.

"You're assuming the worst about someone you haven't even met," Poppy argued.

"You're not listening to me," King Peppy said.

"You're not listening to *me*," Poppy insisted.

King Peppy looked stern. "I'm your father!"

"And I'm the queen!" Poppy countered.

"Father trumps queen!" King Peppy declared. "Now, there's no time to debate this! Let's go. Come along, Branch."

Branch hesitated. He was a big believer in hiding, but he didn't want to go against Poppy. She was frowning.

"We're all Trolls," she said, frustrated by her father's fear. "Differences don't matter."

Later that day, at the edge of the Pop Trolls' village, Poppy tied a pink bow on Queen Barb's bat-creature and sprinkled glitter all over it.

"Look how cute you are!" she exclaimed. She tied a note to the bat-thing's leg. "Barb is going to love your new look! Tell her I look forward to helping her plan the world's biggest party."

Branch came up behind her. "Poppy . . ."

"Ahh!" she yelled, startled.

"What are you doing?" Branch asked, noticing she'd put on a cape.

Poppy tried to look innocent. "Nothing," she said, knowing Branch would disapprove of her plan.

Nearby, Sheila B., a big flower-faced balloon with a basket hanging underneath, was waiting to carry Poppy off on her secret mission. Most of Sheila B.'s flowers were pink, but one of her flower eyes was yellow and the other was blue. Both had red centers. Her mouth was green with green teeth. And her basket was dark green on the outside and purple on the inside.

"Ooh, Poppy's busted!" Sheila B. said, enjoying the little drama.

"Shhhh!" Poppy said, shushing the bigmouthed balloon.

Branch immediately guessed what she was doing. "Sneaking out to meet Barb?" he said. "Heading into enemy territory?"

"She's not the enemy," Poppy insisted. "She's a queen, the same as me." She released the batlike creature, sending it slowly flying over the balloon and into the sky with Poppy's letter to Queen Barb dangling from its leg.

"Bye-bye, little bat!" Sheila B. said, watching it flap its wings, heading for home. Some of Poppy's glitter fluttered down.

"Your dad says Queen Barb is bad news,"

Branch reminded Poppy.

"Well, my dad doesn't know everything."

"He knows more about this!" Branch said, raising his hands in frustration. "You didn't even know there *was* a string until this morning!"

Poppy walked over to the balloon, making adjustments and tossing in gear, including a basket of candy canes and gumdrops. "He may be fine in a world where everybody lives in isolation, but I'm not."

"But we don't know anything about those other Trolls," Branch said.

As they argued, Poppy and Branch didn't notice that Cooper was walking by. He ducked behind a bush and eavesdropped on their conversation. He was curious to find out more about the batlike creature and where it had come from.

"We know they're Trolls," Poppy said simply. "Branch, look around Pop Village. *Everybody's* different. Even us."

Behind his bush, Cooper sneezed. *AH-CHOO!*

Poppy asked. "Did you hear something?"

"Stop trying to change the subject," Branch said.

Poppy started untying the ropes that held the

balloon to the ground. "Being queen means having a lot of power," she said. "And it's my job to use it for good. I can't stay home when I know there is a world out there full of different Trolls, just like us!"

When he heard this, Cooper started getting an idea. He didn't look like any of the other Trolls. His eyes widened as he thought about what Poppy had just said. Different Trolls . . .

"This is a terrible idea that will most likely blow up in your face," Branch warned.

Poppy snipped the last rope, and the flower-faced balloon started to rise. "Okay, bye!" she said from inside the basket.

Branch saw that nothing he said was going to stop Poppy from going ahead with her plan.

"Wait," he said, shooting his hair out to grab a tree limb and flip through the air. He landed in Sheila B.'s basket. "If you aren't going to change your mind, then I guess I'm coming with you."

Poppy breathed a big sigh of relief. "Oh, thank you!" she said gratefully. "I really didn't want to go by myself."

"Oh, yeah," Sheila B. said, excited. "Road trip! Only, you know, in the sky. Without roads."

CHAPTER SEVEN

After the flower-faced balloon had risen into the sky with Poppy and Branch in its basket, Cooper came out from behind the bush. Looking around to see if anyone was watching, he headed back to the grotto where King Peppy had explained the history of the Trolls' musical strings.

Except for the sound of the nearby waterfalls, it was quiet in the grotto, and cool. Cooper crept in and opened the old scroll on the pedestal. He carefully rotated the handles until he came to an illustration showing the Trolls' elders. One of them looked like him!

Cooper gasped. "They *are* all different," he said.

"And this one looks a little bit like me." He leaned in for a closer look. A green leaf fluttered down and landed on the head of the Troll in the drawing. He gasped again. "We even have the same hat!"

That settled it. Cooper hurried home to his pod and dug out his traveling clothes, including a purple cape. He hung his regular hat on a peg labeled EVERYTHING'S GOOD and took the hat from a peg labeled DESTINY HAT. He packed a satchel, careful to include his favorite harmonica. Then he made his way to the edge of Trolls Village and looked back at it sadly.

"Goodbye," he said. "I hope I see you again, friends. But even though it's scary, I have to go out there and see if there are other Trolls like me."

Cooper took a step and almost tumbled down a hill.

"Ahhhh!" He peered over the edge at the wilderness below. "Oh, man, this is gonna be *hard*!"

Queen Barb and her Rockers emerged from the ocean, leaving the undersea world of the Techno Trolls behind. They flew over a bizarre landscape, riding on top of their fishlike creatures, playing and singing a hard-rock song. Barb threw in a squealing guitar solo to bring the song to a close.

"Music has kept us apart—it's time for the rock revolution to start! No spats, no tiffs, no fighting, and everyone's the same!" she roared.

Soon Queen Barb and her fellow Rocker Trolls reached their royal tour bus and went inside. Barb was holding the Techno Trolls' blue string in her fist.

"Yeah!" Barb said triumphantly. "I got the techno string—who knew world domination could be so much fun?"

The Rocker Trolls on the tour bus cheered. Two of them brought a guitar case over to Barb, opening it to reveal a wild-looking guitar with a skull on it. Barb added the techno string to the guitar, putting it next to the rock string. The techno string changed from glowing blue to red, matching the rock string. She grinned, admiring the guitar.

"Only four more strings to go until we unite the world." Then something occurred to her. She raised her head and looked around the tour bus. "Wait—where's Dad?" she asked, turning to the drummer, Riff.

WHOOSH. A flushing sound came from the tour bus's small restroom. The door opened, and an old Rocker Troll in a wheelchair with spikes jutting from the wheels slowly rolled out and parked. It was Barb's father, King Thrash, and he seemed a bit confused, as though his years of listening to loud rock music had scrambled his brains. His black-and-gray hair stood straight up, and his eyes were wide open in a perpetually surprised expression. He smiled vaguely.

"There you are, Dad!" Barb cried, hurrying to his side. "Look! I got the techno string!" She held up the guitar with the new glowing string.

King Thrash spoke, but the words he said were impossible to understand.

"Don't you remember the plan?" Barb asked, somehow figuring out that he didn't know what she was talking about.

The old king mumbled some words—or sounds that may have been words.

"Great idea, man!" Barb said, seeming to understand him. She turned to the other rockers on the bus. "Hey! Line up! We're going to go over the plan again!"

Four Rocker Trolls lined up. As Barb walked past the first one, she said, "Okay. We're on a world tour . . ." The Troll turned around, showing the back of his jacket, which featured a picture of Barb on tour.

". . . and on each stop," Barb continued, "we get a new string!" The second Troll turned around. The back of his jacket showed a map of the six Trolls lands.

"When I have all six strings . . . ," Barb said. The third Troll turned around. The back of her jacket showed Barb onstage at a huge concert venue, holding all six strings in her hand.

". . . and play the ultimate power chord . . . ," she said. The fourth Troll turned around. The back of his jacket showed Barb whaling on her guitar, now equipped with all six strings.

". . . I will unite the Trolls under one music. *Our* music!" she crowed. Everyone on the bus cheered!

King Thrash watched the whole scene with great interest, growing more and more excited. He raised an arm, his fist clenched.

"Here it comes . . . ," Barb said, watching with delight.

Grunting and groaning, King Thrash tried to lift two fingers into the rocker salute. "Ungh! Erngh!"

He couldn't do it.

"Riff, just help him, man," Barb said.

"Yes, Your Rockness," Riff said. He hurried over to the king and helped him open his index finger and pinky finger to make the rocker sign. "Ah, there it is."

"Rock 'n' roll!" the old king rasped.

Everyone cheered!

CHAPTER EIGHT

As the balloon soared past puffy clouds and over colorful, flower-covered hills, Poppy leaned on the edge of the big basket and smiled. What a beautiful world they lived in!

But Branch wasn't admiring the scenery. He pulled a thick owner's manual out of the balloon's glove compartment. "All right. In a short four hundred fifty-six pages, we're gonna know how to fly this thing." He cracked open the massive manual, but Poppy slipped it out of his hands and casually tossed it over the side of the balloon. "HEY!" Branch cried.

"Oh, Branch," Poppy giggled. "We don't need

a giant, comprehensive manual. How hard can it be?" Humming to herself, she chose a button on the complicated control panel at random and pressed it. *ZWOOOOM!* The balloon whizzed through the sky at super speed, blasting through clouds and looping like a roller coaster.

"All right, Poppy," Sheila B. said. "Easy on the buttons."

"Sorry," she said.

ZZZZZZ. A loud snore.

"What was that?" Branch asked, looking around. Poppy hadn't snored. The balloon hadn't snored. And Branch knew *he* hadn't snored.

Following the sound, Poppy leaned down and lifted a tarp. Underneath were Biggie and Mr. Dinkles, asleep. Biggie's face, hands, and body were stained with something pink and sticky. Mr. Dinkles lay across his stomach. "Biggie?" Poppy said.

The big blue Troll woke with a start. He looked up and saw Poppy and Branch staring at him, wondering what he was doing in the balloon. A guilty expression crept over his face. "Oh, hello," he said innocently. "I couldn't help myself. You know how I am around cotton candy."

Poppy had brought lots of cotton candy and other sweets to give to Queen Barb as a present. Biggie stood up with Mr. Dinkles stuck to his stomach. He had trouble peeling his pet worm off, but he did it—and then Mr. Dinkles was stuck to his hand.

"Oh, dear," Biggie said. "Now look what's happened. Mr. Dinkles got all gummed up."

He shook his hand harder and harder, trying to get the worm off. Finally, Mr. Dinkles flew off Biggie's hand . . . and over the side of the balloon's basket!

"Mew!" Mr. Dinkles cried.

"Oh, Mr. Dinkles!" Biggie yelped. "Mr. Dinkles!" He ran to the edge of the basket and peered over. Mr. Dinkles was stuck to the side of the basket. "Oh, there you are." Biggie was relieved. He scooped up his beloved pet. "Right, then, we'll just be on our way."

Looking down, Biggie realized they were far above the ground. "AYYYY!" he screamed. "Poppy, where are you balloon-flying us to?"

"We're on a mission to help Barb unite the Trolls," she explained. "And I'm so glad you're coming with us!"

"I did what in the who, now?" Biggie asked, confused.

Poppy danced over to her supplies. "I hope you didn't eat *all* the cotton candy, because Barb is gonna love it." She started to lift a lid from basket, but Branch quickly slammed it closed.

Poppy realized she'd never seen that particular basket before. "Ahem," she said. "Branchifer, what is this?"

"Oh, it's nothing, nothing, Popifer," Branch said, looking a little embarrassed. "That's just my . . . man stuff."

"I love man stuff!" Poppy cried, lifting the lid. The basket was full of rocks and sharpened sticks. "Weapons?" She was disappointed. "For shame! Violence never solves problems, Branch!"

"I'm not saying we have to use them," Branch argued. "I'm just saying it's better to be prepared in case we need them."

"We won't need them, unless these pointy sticks help you listen," Poppy said. "Or these rocks help you put yourself in someone else's shoes." She picked up a shiny set of brass knuckles and frowned, puzzled. "Is this some kind of jewelry? It's actually kind of cool-looking." Slipping her fingers into the polished brass knuckles, she admired the way they caught the sunlight. She sang a high note to go with their gleam. "Ooohhh!"

Branch reached for the brass knuckles. "Give me those! We don't even know what's out there!"

Before Branch could stop her, Poppy dumped the basket of weapons over the side of the balloon. "Wait!" Branch cried. "No! I whittled those for hours!"

"Branch, the only weapons we need are this guy"—she made a fist and touched her bicep—"and this guy!" She made another fist, showing her other bicep while also making a fierce face. Then she grinned and opened her arms wide. "For hugs!"

Biggie was looking over the edge of the basket at the ground below. "Poppy," he said in a worried voice, "you may want to see this."

Poppy and Branch looked over the side of the basket and saw the smoldering ruins of another Trolls village.

"This is going to take a lot of hugs," Branch grimly muttered to himself.

CHAPTER NINE

The buildings in the village had the shapes and curves of musical instruments—instruments that had been blasted and broken. The balloon came in for a landing, and Poppy, Branch, and Biggie climbed out of the basket to explore the site of devastation.

As they carefully picked their way through the village's smashed remains, Poppy wondered just what she had gotten them into.

"Whoa," Branch said. "Something gnarly happened here."

"Hello?" said a high-pitched voice, sounding scared.

They looked around but didn't see anyone.

"Who said that?" Branch asked. "Identify yourself!"

"Are you nice or are you mean?" the voice asked.

"We're nice," Poppy assured the unseen speaker. "We're really nice."

"But not *too* nice," Branch added. "So don't even try it!" He didn't trust anyone he couldn't see. Or lots of creatures he *could* see.

"Okay," the little voice said hesitantly. A frightened little musical instrument, kind of like a piccolo, emerged from the shadows. Her name was Pennywhistle. She was gold-colored, with finger holes and long eyelashes.

"What is this place?" Poppy asked gently, not wanting to scare the little instrument away.

"It used to be called Symphonyville, where the Classical Trolls lived," Pennywhistle explained. "That was in the Before."

"What happened here?" Poppy asked.

"Well," Pennywhistle said, "Symphonyville was the most wonderful place you ever did see. It was a place where all of the Classical Trolls could live in perfect harmony." As she looked at the remnants of her village, Pennywhistle recalled what it used to be like.

"Wherever the conductor led, we followed," she said, picturing the small Classical Troll with curls of white hair piled high on his head who kept their musical string hidden inside his baton. "His name was Trollzart, and he loved telling us, 'Play! Play! Beautiful!' "

Pennywhistle smiled, thinking of the wonderful music they'd all made together. But her smile turned to a frown. "Then Queen Barb showed up with her Rock army. 'What's up, Trollzart dude?' she said. 'I'm here for your string!' "

"Queen Barb?" Poppy asked.

Pennywhistle nodded. "Conductor Trollzart told her we would not go quietly, and started to conduct us in a symphonic attack. But Queen Barb blasted us with a rock guitar chord! The conductor fell to the ground and dropped his baton. Queen Barb picked it up, snapped it in half, and pulled out our string."

Poppy and Branch looked stunned. For a moment, Pennywhistle just shook her head, overcome by the sad memories. Then she took a deep breath and said, "She took our string, our music. She took everyone. We lost everything."

"Barb doesn't want to unite us," Poppy said, realizing the truth. "She wants to destroy us."

Branch steeled himself. "We need to make sure our own string is safe."

"Our string *is* safe," Poppy said, pulling the glowing pink string out of her hair. It made a beautiful sound.

Branch couldn't believe what he was seeing and hearing.

"What?" he shouted. "Poppy, are you crazy? Carrying the Pop Trolls' string around in your *hair*?"

She looked a little embarrassed. "I thought it was a good idea at the time," she admitted. "I can't believe another queen would use her power for evil."

"Okay, change of plans," Branch said, heading back toward the balloon. "We need to get home as fast as we can and get in the bunker."

Poppy stopped him. "Uh, no. Change of plans. We have to stop Barb from destroying all music."

CHAPTER TEN

Branch stared at her in disbelief. "Can you just look at reality this one time?"

"Branch, I am!" Poppy insisted. "If I don't stop Barb, who will?"

Branch shook his head. He didn't have a good answer for Poppy's question, but he wasn't at all happy about the idea of the three of them taking on Queen Barb's army of Rocker Trolls. Looking around, he could see what the Rocker Trolls had done to Symphonyville with their blasts of deafening rock. He worried about the damage Barb and her army might have planned for Trolls Village. He didn't want to go any farther. He wanted to make sure he and his friends were safe.

"Poppy," Biggie said, speaking up for the first time since they'd arrived at the scene of destruction, "you said this could be handled with hugs! How are we going to hug our way out of this one?" He was very upset by what they were seeing.

Poppy touched his arm. "It's okay, Biggie," she reassured him.

"Really?" Biggie said, scared. "It's okay to be terrified?" He shook his head. "When am I going to learn to stay away from the cotton candy?"

"As your queen, I promise I will protect you, no matter what." She could see that Biggie still wasn't convinced. She got an idea. "I pinky promise," she said in a deadly serious voice, holding up her pinky.

Biggie gasped. "Poppy, you know you can't go back on a pinky promise!"

"Never did, never will," Poppy said firmly.

Biggie looked at Mr. Dinkles, who nodded. The big Troll offered his bent pinky to Poppy, and they hooked their pinky fingers together. *BOOOOOM!* A shock wave spread out from the sheer power of the pinky promise. The ground shook, and a column of bright light shone into the sky.

In a forest, Cooper crossed a wide clearing, still wearing his traveling cape and hat. He felt a *WHOOSH* as the mighty tremor from Poppy and Biggie's pinky promise swept through the woods. He looked up in the sky and saw the column of light in the distance.

"A pinky promise!" he exclaimed to himself. "Dang!"

He walked on, determined to find other Trolls like himself somewhere.

Back in the ruins of Symphonyville, the wind died down. The pinky promise was complete. "Let it be so," Poppy said formally.

"And so it is," Biggie responded, following the ritual of the pinky promise.

"This just got real," Pennywhistle said in a voice filled with awe.

Poppy turned to Branch. "You're right. I can't do this alone."

Branch was touched. Not only was Poppy admitting he was right, she was also saying she couldn't stop Barb without him.

Then she whipped out a felt map of the Trolls Kingdom that she'd made herself, based on the ancient scroll her father had shown them, and unrolled it. It showed all six Trolls lands—the woodsy village of the Pop Trolls, the undersea kingdom of the Techno Trolls, the now ruined Symphonyville, the desert realm of the Country Western Trolls, the mysterious dwelling of the Funk Trolls, and the forbidding volcano island of the Rocker Trolls.

Poppy placed red, blue, and green candies on three of the lands. "We need the others—the Country Western, Techno, and Funk Trolls." She used a candy cane to push all the candies together into one pile while chewing a piece of gum herself. "Then we'll face Barb as a united alliance. We need to remind her that she's one of us."

She blew a big bubble and popped it with determination. *POP!*

"YEE!" Biggie yelped, still on edge.

Poppy turned to Pennywhistle. "We have to get to the Country Western Trolls in Lonesome Flats before Barb does. Will you come with us?"

"Oh, no," Pennywhistle said, shaking her head. "Someone has to rebuild Symphonyville. Pennywhistle is the woodwind for the job."

Poppy nodded, understanding the desire to fix one's broken home. She put a tiny hard hat on the determined little instrument. "Good luck, little Pennywhistle."

"Goodbye, Poppy," she said bravely. Grunting, she pushed a small rock onto another rock. It tumbled off.

Pennywhistle sighed.

CHAPTER ELEVEN

Barb's delivery bat flapped into the Rocker Trolls' tour bus wearing the bow and glitter from Poppy. When Barb saw it, she said, "What is that thing?"

She looked closer at the colorful creature.

"Wait, is that Debbie? What did they do to you, my hairy little baby? Come here, come here." Debbie flew over to Barb, who found Poppy's card attached to her leg. "What is this? Something from the Pop Trolls?"

She removed the envelope from Debbie's leg and opened the flap, then pulled out the sparkly card and read it. "'Dear Barb, Can't wait to meet you! I have tons of great party ideas. Maybe you and I can even be best friends!' "

"Party ideas," King Thrash mumbled, smiling. "I like that!"

Barb turned to Riff. "Best friends? Wait, is she making fun of me? No one says that! 'Cause friendship takes time and years of mutual care and respect! You don't just become best friends! Plus, everyone knows that I already have a ton of friends! Like Carol!" Barb pointed toward a Rocker Troll lying in the corner. "Right, Carol?"

Carol didn't say anything. She just squirted cheese out of can straight into her mouth. Some shot back out her nose.

"Okay, you're busy," Barb said. "That's fine. Love you, Carol."

Barb heard a hissing sound like a lit fuse. *SSSSS* . . . She looked down and saw that it was coming from Poppy's card. *POOF!* Glitter shot out of the card, spraying Barb in the face, while a few notes of a catchy pop song played.

"Gnarly," Riff commented.

Furious at being covered in glitter, Barb growled and started smashing up the tour bus. "Pop music isn't even *real* music!" she snarled, using a chain saw to cut a sofa in half. "It's bland! It's repetitive! The lyrics are empty! Worst of all, it crawls into your head like an earworm! You can't get it out!"

She paused her tantrum, catching her breath. "Oohh," she said, gasping for air. "I'm tired now. Hating things takes a lot of energy."

Distracted, King Thrash hummed the tune from the card. Barb ran over to her father and knelt by his side, concerned. "Oh, no! Look what their music just did to Dad! Daddy? Come back! Come back to me, Daddy!"

She gave him a juice box and kissed his forehead. Then she picked up Poppy's card from the floor of the tour bus. "No one makes fun of Queen Barb! We need to find this Queen Poppy and her string. And I know *exactly* who to ask to find her!"

It didn't take Barb long to round up three teams of bounty hunters to search for Poppy. First there was Chaz, who played smooth jazz on his saxophone, lulling his victims into a trancelike state. Second, the Reggaeton Trolls, who loved reggaeton music. And third, the K-Pop Gang, who sang and danced to K-pop music as they captured their prey.

They lined up in front of Queen Barb, and she paced before them, giving them their orders. "You are the most feared bounty hunters in all of Trolldom," she said. "Whoever brings me Queen Poppy gets to keep their music after I unite the Trolls world as one. Everyone else will lose theirs forever. Okay . . . go! What are you all standing around for? Get me Queen Poppy!"

As the bounty hunters filed out, heading off to find Poppy, Barb noticed that one of the teams she'd summoned hadn't shown up. "Hey, Riff," she asked. "Where are the Yodelers?"

"I heard a rumor they yodeled so hard, an avalanche fell on 'em," Riff said.

Barb wasn't interested in rumors. "Well, I don't pay you to hear!"

"Actually, I'm doing this for college credit," Riff replied nonchalantly. Riff was always kind of mellow—except when he was ROCKING, of course!

"If anyone can find me Queen Poppy and her string, it's the Yodelers," Barb said. She held Poppy's card over a burning candle and it burst into flames. *FWOOF!* A last little spray of glitter puffed out. A felt image of Poppy's face on the cover of the card started to burn until it became ash and blew away.

As the sun rose the next morning, Poppy, Branch, and Biggie reached the top of a rocky desert mesa. They spotted a cluster of buildings not too far off.

"According to the map," Branch said, "that's it. That's Lonesome Flats, where the Country Western Trolls live."

"Great!" Poppy said. "Let's get down there!"

They scrambled down the mesa to the flat desert below and made their way along an open road, past two huge cacti, and into the country western town just as a clock struck six o'clock. Passing a sign that read WELCOME TO LONESOME FLATS, they entered the small town's main street.

The mayor of Lonesome Flats, Delta Dawn, walked out of City Hall. She had big red hair with a little white cowboy hat pinned to it, a white body with four legs like a horse, a green plaid top, and a long, green tail.

"Mornin', Delta Dawn," a Country Western Troll said.

The mayor nodded and began singing a lonesome Country Western tune about how hard life could be. During the song, a newly hatched baby Troll was put right to work. Life was tough! The Country Western Trolls loved to get their day started with a sad, sad song.

Poppy was ready to run straight up and start talking to Mayor Delta Dawn, but Branch pulled her and Biggie back. He wanted to spy on the Country Western Trolls for a few moments to plan their approach. Biggie hid inside a barrel in an alley, and Mr. Dinkles peeked out a hole in it. Poppy and Branch peered around from behind the barrel. As the Pop Trolls listened to the Country Western Trolls' morning song, they grew confused. These earth-toned Trolls were totally new to the Pop Trolls.

"This song is so sad!" Poppy said. As they watched, one of the Country Western Trolls started to cry softly, moved by Delta Dawn's mournful song. A tear rolled down his cheek. Then even the tear started to cry.

"Yeah," Branch said. "This song is sad, but life is sad sometimes, so . . . I kinda like it."

Poppy looked surprised. "You do? But it's so

different! These Country Western Trolls must not know that music's supposed to make you happy. That's awful!"

The Country Western Trolls of Lonesome Flats joined Delta Dawn in singing their sad song and went about their morning chores.

Just as Delta Dawn ended the song, she and her sidekick, Growly Pete, had spotted Poppy, Branch, and Biggie huddled in the alley. Twirling his long green mustache between his fingers, Growly Pete growled suspiciously.

"Now, take it easy, Growly Pete," Mayor Delta Dawn said. "I feel bad for them. Looks like they got beat up by a rainbow. Let's give 'em a chance."

Growly Pete reluctantly agreed. But he didn't like it.

In their huddle, Poppy told Branch and Biggie, "Guys, first things first. These Trolls need some serious cheering up. Gonna have to go top-shelf."

Branch and Biggie gasped. "When you say 'top-shelf,'" Branch asked, "you don't mean . . . ?"

"That's right," Poppy confirmed, nodding. "We need to sing them the most important songs in the history of music."

"Yes, but which ones?" Biggie asked.

Poppy got a determined look on her face. "All of them."

Branch and Biggie let this sink in. Then Branch asked, "And when you say 'all of them,' you don't mean . . ."

But Poppy had already leapt onto a bandstand and started singing a medley of cheerful pop music. She wore purple leg warmers, a striped dress, and yellow heart-shaped glasses.

Biggie jumped in, dancing and singing with her. He wore heart-shaped glasses, too, but also red track pants, a red vest, and a big gold *B* on his chest. Strapped to Biggie's back, Mr. Dinkles barked a call-and-response. He wore a new green cap.

Overcoming any misgivings he'd had about Poppy's plan to cheer up the Country Western Trolls, Branch joined them, busting out some sweet dance moves that were all his own. His heart-shaped glasses had yellow frames and purple lenses.

All the Country Western Trolls just stared at the dancing, singing Pop Trolls. Instead of cheering them up, the medley of bright, bouncy tunes seemed to be making them angry.

Poppy, Branch, and Biggie didn't notice the Country Western Trolls' negative reaction as they launched into another song-and-dance routine.

The Country Western Trolls scowled.

Biggie switched to a different song again.

The Country Western Trolls glared. A few of them shook their heads and stamped their feet.

The Pop Trolls finished their medley with a flourish, tossing glitter in the air and striking a pose.

Silence. A tumbleweed rolled by and yelled, "You suck!"

Moments later . . . *CLANG!*

A jail cell door slammed shut, imprisoning Poppy, Branch, Biggie, and Mr. Dinkles!

CHAPTER TWELVE

Delta Dawn turned the key in the jail door, locking it. "Now, I want you to sit in here and think about what you've just done," she told the Pop Trolls through the bars. "That was a crime against music!"

The mayor and Growly Pete turned to leave, but Poppy called out to them, "Wait, no! We're here to warn you about Barb, the Queen of Rock!"

Smiling, Delta Dawn turned back to the cell. "Sweetie, I already know and have heard about this Queen Barb and her fancy world tour."

Poppy shook her head. "No, you don't understand," she insisted. "She's stealing everyone's strings. She wants to destroy all music except her own. We need to band together and remind her she's the same as us."

Delta Dawn looked offended. "We are *not* the same, honey," she disagreed. "I'd *never* do what you just did to music. Now, if you'll excuse me, I gotta go wash out my ears. With soap."

A little Country Western Troll with pigtails and huge teeth peeked out from the mayor's big hair. "Oh, you're in *real* trouble now!" Clampers Buttonwillow crowed. "Right, Aunt Delta?"

"Keep an eye on 'em, Growly Pete," Delta Dawn told her sidekick as she left the jail.

"Yeah, stinkin' pop music!" Clampers sneered. "Nasty!"

As Delta Dawn walked away, Poppy called after her again. "No! Music should bring us together, not divide us!" But this time, the mayor just kept walking. Poppy kicked a rock on the floor in frustration.

"Okay, Branch," Poppy said to him, plopping down on a cot. "You can say 'I told you so.'"

Instead, Branch sat next to Poppy to comfort her. "I can, but I won't. Because that's not what you do to . . . friends. You did great out there, Poppy."

She looked up at him, grateful for his comforting words. They smiled at each other.

Okay. This was it. Branch could feel that this was the moment. He could finally tell Poppy how he felt about her. He took a deep breath, and—*CRASH!*

Biggie, who had been cowering in the rafters, fell from a broken beam, landing right between the two of them. "I'll never survive the big house," he said anxiously. "We've got to get out of here."

"I know," Poppy said, giving him a reassuring pat. "That was such a rad medley. I can't believe it didn't work!"

"Tell me about it," Biggie complained. "I did the splits and no one even clapped. Am I not cute anymore? Come on!" What he didn't realize was that his purple shorts were now torn in back, revealing his blue bottom.

"Maybe if we started with a different song?" Poppy speculated. "Or maybe it was our dance moves. Or maybe we didn't use enough glitter?"

Branch looked exasperated. "Or *maybe* the other Trolls aren't into our music because they're different."

Poppy thought about this possibility. "Maybe

my dad was right," she said slowly. "The other Trolls are different in ways I was not prepared for." Then she realized something incredible and appalling. "Some Trolls—they *don't* just want to have fun!"

They sat in the cell for a moment, silently thinking about this gloomy possibility. Then Mr. Dinkles spoke up. "Anybody got a Plan B?"

Branch pointed to his head. "Plan B is up here. Step One: escape from Lonesome Flats!" He examined the floor of the cell and found that it was dirt. Reaching into his hair, he pulled out a foldable shovel. "Travel shovel," he explained.

He started digging an escape tunnel. Biggie helped, using Mr. Dinkles as a second shovel. The big worm scooped dirt in his mouth and spat it out.

"PTOOEY! PTOOEY!"

Poppy looked around the cell, wishing there were some other option. But she couldn't come up with one. "Plan B it is," she sighed. As she searched for something to help dig with . . .

TWANG! A lasso wrapped around the bars of the locked cell door. *CRRRRASH!* It yanked the door, and the wall crumbled into rubble and dust!

CHAPTER THIRTEEN

When the dust cleared, the Pop Trolls saw a Country Western Troll holding the other end of the rope that had set them free. He had long sideburns, a red tail, and a big white cowboy hat that was almost as tall as he was. Like the other Country Western Trolls, he also had four legs with hooves.

"It ain't right to put you in jail just 'cause your music's different," he drawled. "Seems some folks around here don't appreciate a rad medley when they hear one. Let's skedaddle!" He extended his hand.

"Yes!" Poppy exclaimed, pumping her fist in triumph. "Mission back on!" She jumped up and grabbed the Country Western Troll's hand.

"Poppy!" Branch cried. "You don't even know who this is!"

Poppy looked at the stranger. "I'm Queen Poppy," she said. "What's your name?"

"Name's Hickory," he replied. "Hop on!"

Poppy turned to Branch. "Branch, this is Hickory." She turned back to the Country Western Troll. "Hickory, this is Branch." She hopped on Hickory's back for a ride, holding on to his hat.

"Enough with the formalities," Biggie said hurriedly, climbing onto the cell door, which was still attached to Hickory's lasso. "Let's go!" Then he remembered that he hadn't introduced his pet. "This is Mr. Dinkles, by the way."

"Let's skedaddle!" Hickory repeated. "*Hieeeyah!*" He took off running with Poppy on his back and Biggie on the jail door dragging behind them like a sled. Branch still hesitated, unhappy about trusting a complete stranger.

Delta Dawn saw Poppy and Biggie getting away. "Go git 'em, Clampers!" she ordered, dropping the little Country Western Troll on the ground. Clampers sped off after the escaping Trolls, gnashing her big white teeth, eager to bite!

When Branch saw the Country Music Troll coming, he quickly made up his mind, sprinting after Hickory, Poppy, and Biggie. "This is my Plan C, by the way!" he exclaimed. He caught up and leapt onto the skidding jail door next to Biggie and Mr. Dinkles.

"Charge!" Delta Dawn commanded. She and several other Country Western Trolls chased after Hickory and the Pop Trolls, tearing across the desert landscape.

Looking over her shoulder, Poppy saw that the Country Western Trolls were gaining on them. "Oh, no, Hickory!" she shouted.

"I got it, Queen Poppy!" he said, heading for an old pit mine in the dry earth. He easily leapt over the mine, but Champers plunged into it.

"YAAAAHHH!" she cried.

The other Country Western Trolls just kept coming. "Come on, Growly Pete," Delta Dawn said. "Do your thing!"

Growly Pete twirled his long green mustache into two lassos and sent them flying at the Pop Trolls. "No one can escape my mustache!"

One of the mustache lassos snagged Branch's leg, yanking him off the jail door! "AHHHH!" he screamed. Then he started laughing. "The mustache tickles!"

Growly Pete dug in his heels and pulled his head back, trying to wrench Branch over to the Country Western Trolls. Branch grabbed for Biggie's hand, but instead got ahold of Mr. Dinkles's head!

"Branch!" Biggie yelled. "Hold on to Mr. Dinkles!"

Branch held on. As Growly Pete pulled on his mustache lasso, Mr. Dinkles got stretched longer and longer.

"Meweeeeeee!" Mr. Dinkles chirped.

Clampers tunneled through the ground, burst from the earth, and launched herself through the air, her mouth open wide and her teeth spinning like a buzz saw. *CHOMP!* She clamped her teeth on Branch's pants and tugged at them.

"YEEEAAAH!" Branch screamed, barely managing to hold on to Mr. Dinkles's tiny top hat with two fingers.

Hickory and the Pop Trolls whipped past some hairy cattle with long striped horns calmly chewing their cud. First came Hickory, galloping furiously, with Poppy holding on for dear life. Behind them stretched his rope, which was still tied to the jailhouse door. Biggie clung to the door as it bounced over the desert floor, kicking up dust. He also held on to Mr. Dinkles, who was stretched way behind the door. Branch brought up the rear, clinging to Mr. Dinkles as Clampers yanked at his pants.

"Okay, y'all," Delta Dawn called to her posse, "flank 'em!"

The Country Western Trolls closed in on both sides of the Pop Trolls.

"AAAHH!" Poppy cried.

"Hold on!" Hickory told her.

But Poppy looked ahead, peering over Hickory's shoulder, and saw that they were rapidly approaching the edge of a cliff! "We're not gonna make it!" she cried.

"Oh, yes we are!" Branch assured her. He grabbed Clampers and used her sharp teeth to bite through Growly Pete's mustache lasso. Freed from the mustache, Branch shot forward. Mr. Dinkles snapped back to his normal length and bumped into Biggie, who slammed into Hickory, knocking

Poppy off her perch. They all screamed as they flew over the edge of the cliff.

"YAAAAAHHHH!"

As they hung suspended over the canyon for just a second, Hickory said, "Well, I hope Pop Trolls can swim!"

Then they plummeted toward the rushing water at the bottom of the ravine!

CHAPTER FØURTEEN

Delta Dawn and her fellow Country Western Trolls peered over the edge of the cliff, unwilling to follow the Pop Trolls down into the raging rapids far below. The mayor threw her little cowboy hat on the ground in frustration. "Well, dangity-doodly."

Clampers spit on the ground, equally frustrated. Then she climbed back into Delta Dawn's big hair, and they headed back to town.

Mr. Dinkles imagined he was flying up into the sky toward big, fluffy clouds that looked like tasty pink cotton candy. The clouds parted, and a huge majestic figure appeared. The figure looked like him, but he had a long white beard and mustache and wore a golden crown. In his hand was a royal scepter. A bright light shone behind his head, and gentle music played. The huge figure smiled benevolently down at him.

"Mew," Mr. Dinkles said when he saw the friendly being.

"Welcome home," the personage said in a deep, warm voice.

Then Mr. Dinkles stopped floating upward— he fell back toward Earth!

"Mew!" he cried.

On a riverbank, Biggie was reviving Mr. Dinkles with mouth-to-mouth resuscitation. He pressed on his pet's body, and river water fountained out of Mr. Dinkles's mouth. *GLURG!*

"Oh, Mr. Dinkles!" Biggie cried, relieved. "You're alive! For a minute there, I thought you'd kicked the bucket."

He hugged his pet worm, overjoyed.

Meanwhile, Poppy was clinging to the riverbank, the rapids churning just below her dangling bare feet. "Help! Branch! AAAHHH!"

"Poppy, hang on!" Branch called to her. "I got you!"

ZHWWWIP! Branch whipped his hair to Poppy and pulled her up. They collapsed to the ground.

"You do got me," Poppy said. "You always got me."

"I'm so glad you're all right," Branch said.

"Thanks to you," Poppy said, smiling.

"That's what friends are for, right?" Branch asked.

"Yeah," Poppy agreed.

They looked at each other for a moment. Then . . . *SPLAT!* Water sprayed all over Branch, soaking him. Hickory was shaking the river water off his body.

"Whoo-ee!" Hickory whooped, shaking off more water.

"There you are!" Poppy called, happy to see him.

"I think we lost 'em," Hickory said. "We should be all right."

"Thank you!" Poppy said, standing up. "I don't know how we can repay you. Oh, wait!" She held up a heaping handful of gumdrops. "Yes, I do know . . . gumdrops!"

She put the gumdrops into Hickory's hand.

"Gum-what?" he said, unfamiliar with the candy. "Oh, well, thank you." He popped one into his mouth and chewed. "That's got a zing, don't it?"

"It's not candy time!" Branch argued, popping an irresistible gumdrop into his own mouth. "It's *question* time!" He wanted to know more about Hickory before they went any farther with him. But then . . .

DING! Poppy and Biggie's Hug Time bracelets chimed.

"Hug Time!" Poppy said.

"Hug Time!" Biggie agreed.

They all went in for a group hug. Branch was the first to break out of it. He wanted to get back to questioning Hickory. "Why are you helping us?" he demanded. "What's in it for you?"

Poppy couldn't believe Branch was asking Hickory accusing questions right after he'd helped them escape the other Country Western Trolls.

"Branch!" she said sharply. She turned to Hickory. "I'm sorry about my associate."

But Hickory didn't mind Branch's questions. "I loved your message about music bringing Trolls together," the cowboy said. "Delta Dawn shoulda listened to you."

Poppy nodded. "I know! If we never see past our differences, we'll never be able to realize that we're all the same!"

"You're darn skippy," Hickory agreed. "You may be Pop, and I may be Country, but Trolls is Trolls."

Poppy shot Branch a look that said, "See? I was right!"

But Branch rolled his eyes, unimpressed. " 'Trolls *is* Trolls.' Wow. Deep. I'm gonna have to go ponder that one by a stream."

Poppy shot another look at Branch, one that clearly said "Be nice!" Then she turned back to Hickory. "This is the beginning of a partnership between Trolls that's going to save *all* Trolls." Holding up her map, she turned to Branch and Biggie. "Okay," she continued, "we need to get to the Funk Trolls before Queen Barb does."

Hickory stroked his chin, thinking. "Well," he drawled, "the quickest way is down that river. I'll build us a raft." He headed off into the scrub brush to gather the materials he needed.

Branch looked smug. "This oughta be good. That guy probably doesn't know the first thing about building a raft."

But in no time at all, Hickory put together an incredibly elaborate wooden raft. It had two levels, with ladders leading up to the top level, where the steering wheel was. At the front of the lower level was a stone ring for campfires at night. Hickory lowered the raft's handmade canopy and nodded toward the cappuccino maker. "Cappuccino, anyone?" he offered.

Poppy smiled gleefully and answered, "Cappuccino? Cappucci-*YES!*"

Branch narrowed his eyes and replied, "I do want one. But I'm not happy about it." He sighed and motioned for Hickory to make one for him as well.

Meanwhile, not far away, Cooper continued his journey through the unknown lands, looking for signs of life. Stopping for a moment to catch his breath and take in the wonders of the countryside, he spotted something familiar. Two sets of blue legs! As far as he knew, he was the only Troll with four legs.

"Trolls that look like me," he whispered to himself.

He approached the legs quickly but cautiously. When he got closer, he realized that the legs didn't belong to Trolls. They belonged to some strange honking birds. As the birds bobbed up and down, they made noises that sounded like a horn section. One of them grabbed Cooper in its beak, and Cooper immediately pooped out cupcakes, each with a lit birthday candle. After pulling free of the bird, Cooper offered the cupcakes to the creatures.

"Happy birthday," he said.

CHAPTER FIFTEEN

That day, they made their way down the river on Hickory's custom-built raft, heading toward the land of the Funk Trolls. By nightfall, they'd passed out of the desert and into a lush swamp. Trees along the banks were covered in drooping moss. A cool breeze blew. Water lapped at the shore.

Hickory built a fire with Biggie's help. Glowing sparks soon rose into the starry sky.

"It is a nice night, isn't it?" Biggie said. "Mr. Dinkles loves a full moon."

"Let's get our grub on," Hickory said, stirring a pot he'd hung over the small fire. "Who's ready?"

"I'll put on more kindlin'," Poppy said in a

Country Western accent.

Branch took Poppy aside for a confidential talk at the other end of the raft. "Maybe it's just me," he said quietly, "but are you getting a weird vibe from Hickory?"

Poppy looked surprised. "What? *No.* Why? Are you?"

"I just don't trust him." Branch said.

By the campfire, Biggie and Hickory sat eating.

"That's good grub," said Hickory. "What do you think?"

Too polite to answer with his mouth full, Biggie nodded enthusiastically.

Nearby, in the water, someone was spying on them, breathing through something that looked like a reed. . . a reed *instrument.* . . .

On the raft, Poppy considered what Branch had just told her about not trusting Hickory. "Yeah," she said, "but you don't trust anybody, Branch. He doesn't have an ulterior motive. The guy rescued us and built us this incredible raft."

Rolling his eyes, Branch replied, "He hasn't done anything I couldn't do."

"Except be cool," Poppy teased. "Am I right?"

"I'm cool!" Branch protested. Then he realized insisting he was cool probably wasn't very cool. "Whatever. I just want us to be safe. You know what's not cool or safe? Putting too much trust in a complete stranger."

Poppy looked offended. "Oh, I see," she replied coolly. "It's not Hickory you don't trust. It's me! You don't think I'm a good queen?"

Flustered by Poppy's accusation, Branch sputtered, "Wait, what? I didn't say that. Why are you trying to make this into such a big deal?"

"I thought we were friends, Branch," Poppy said, hurt. "I'm starting to think you don't even know what that means."

Branch leaned in, speaking intensely. "We *are* friends! Sometimes that means speaking up if I think *you* are making a mistake."

Their argument was interrupted by the sound of smooth jazz filling the air. Bright, swirly orbs of light, like the blobs that pulse inside a lava lamp, floated in front of Poppy, Branch, Biggie, and Mr. Dinkles.

"Did you hear something?" Poppy asked.

Chaz, Barb's bounty hunter, rose out of the water and floated up through the fog, playing hypnotic music on his saxophone. Candles and shiny bubbles floated on the river. Petals filled the air. Magical butterflies fluttered out of his horn. He had long hair and a mustache.

Staring at Chaz, entranced by his smooth music, Poppy murmured, "Look at that guy's chest hair. . . ."

"Poppy," Branch said in a dreamy voice, "I can't feel my face. . . ."

"It's like I'm being paralyzed by the music's smoothness," Poppy managed to say, just before she began to gently sway to the rhythm of the tune. Branch was firmly in the grip of Chaz's jazz, too. It carried them into a fantasy. . . .

In space, Poppy and Branch sat together on a moonlit beach. A white tiger flew around, roaring, but it didn't frighten them. A guy walked in and poured them two glasses of fizzy blue juice from little boxes. They toasted with their glasses. CLINK!

An old-fashioned phone appeared, ringing. BRRING-RING! BRRING-RING! *Poppy picked up the receiver and said, "Hello?"*

"Hello," Branch said on the other end of the line. "It's me! Look . . . narwhals!"

He pointed out into the ocean. Narwhals with long tusks jumped out of the sea, trailing silvery sprays of water behind them.

"Totally nar-nar," Poppy said in a blissful voice. The white tiger looked on with shining green eyes.

Biggie rode by on a narwhal with Mr. Dinkles balanced just behind its tusk. "Poppy!" he said to her, waving.

Then Poppy and Branch imagined that they were two pieces of sushi on a plate. They both started eating a sushi roll, Poppy nibbling at one end while Branch ate from the other. They held the roll with chopsticks. . . .

BOP! BOP! BOP! In reality, Branch was tapping Poppy's tongue with a stick. "Poppy, how do you like the sushi?" he asked dreamily.

CLUNK. A key turned in a heavy lock, trapping Biggie, Mr. Dinkles, Branch, and Poppy in a cage. Biggie and his pet worm had been entranced, too. Now the friends snapped out of it.

"What happened?" Poppy asked.

"Got ya, pop babies!" Chaz crowed. "Soon Queen Barb is going to have your string, and the world will be rid of cheesy, pointless pop music once and for all!"

"Hold it right there, Chaz!" Hickory barked, jumping toward them and landing between the Smooth Jazz Troll and his caged captives.

Chaz looked confused. "And who are you supposed to be, Cowboy Pants?"

"Name's Hickory," he said, touching his hat, "and I don't much care for smooth jazz."

"Oh, yeah?" Chaz said. "Well, you've never had the Chaz experience." He whipped out his saxophone and started to play his hypnotically smooth music. But he'd only gotten out a few notes, when . . . *WHAM!* Hickory kicked Chaz off the raft and into the river. *SPLOOSH!*

Hickory pulled two gumdrops from his ears, one green and one blue. He'd used them to block Chaz's hypnotic tune. "Gumdrops—soundproof and delicious!" He popped them into his mouth.

Chaz surfaced, shouting at the raft as the current swiftly swept him away. "You'll never get away with this!" he threatened. "Queen Barb will find you! Smooth jazz will be heard again! Smooth jazz will never die!"

CHAPTER SIXTEEN

As Hickory released them from the cage, Poppy and Branch looked shaken. "Who was that guy?" Poppy asked.

"One of the many bounty hunters out there looking for you," Hickory answered.

"That was awful!" Biggie cried, remembering the music. "So smooth and easy and awful!"

Hickory patted his shoulder. "I know, big buddy," he said comfortingly. "It's enough to put you off jazz altogether."

Biggie took in a deep breath and let it out. Then he got a determined look on his face. "All right, that's it," he announced. "We need to go home."

"Biggie, it'll be okay," Poppy reassured him.

"Stop saying that and listen to me!" Biggie said. "You only hear what you want to hear, and it puts us all in danger! How are you supposed to save the world if you can't even keep us safe?"

Poppy was stunned. Biggie was right. She hadn't saved them from Chaz's music, and they'd ended up locked in a cage. If it hadn't been for Hickory sticking gumdrops in his ears, they'd *still* be in a cage.

"You made a pinky promise to me, Queen Poppy," Biggie reminded her, "and you broke it." He made a decision. Pulling Mr. Dinkles' hat like a cord, he started him up like a motorboat. *PUH-PUH-PUH-PUH-PRROOOM!* Biggie leaned over, placed Mr. Dinkles in the water, and stepped onto his back. Biggie rode his pet worm across the water to the riverbank with his arms crossed, yelling back, "What kind of queen breaks a pinky promise?"

"Biggie, no!" Poppy cried after him, heartbroken to see him go.

Cooper stumbled step by step through the desert. He was hot, tired, and thirsty. As far as he could see, there was nothing but glittering, golden sand.

"So hot . . . ," said the sun burning down on the weary Troll.

Then Cooper spotted something shining in the distance. A pool of water! Cool, refreshing water! He gathered all his energy and ran toward it.

When he reached the pool of clear blue water, he looked at his reflection. "I'm saved!" he said joyfully. He lowered his head with his long neck and started drinking in huge gulps.

"Are you really saved?" his reflection asked. "Because last I checked, I was a mirage!"

POOF! The pool of water disappeared, replaced by sand dunes. Cooper spat out the sand he'd been scooping into his mouth. "PLEEAAAH!"

He looked around. Nothing but empty desert for as far as he could see. "I'm done for!" he croaked. "And on top of that, I never found any Trolls like me!" He swooned and collapsed on the sand.

Slowly, a shadow covered him. Something large was passing between Cooper and the sun— something big. Then . . . *FWOOM!* A bright light shone down. A bubble surrounded him, knocking off his Destiny hat, and he was lifted into the air, trapped inside the bubble!

"AAAHHH!" Cooper screamed. "NOOOO!"

A second bubble came down and lifted up his hat.

"Whoa!" said the sun.

The bubble carried Cooper into the observation room of a huge, shiny spaceship. *POP!* The bubble broke, and Cooper fell onto the cool chrome floor. *THUD!*

Cooper looked up, but twinkling bright lights were shining in his face, so he couldn't see. He shaded his eyes, squinting. Two tall silhouettes loomed over him.

"Q, is that . . . ?" a female voice asked. "I think our search is finally over!"

Overjoyed, Cooper beamed at who he saw standing in front of him.

The next day, Poppy steered the raft down the river, past cattail plants growing along the banks. She felt sad thinking about Biggie and how he'd said she'd failed as his queen.

Poppy is Queen of the Trolls. She can't stop singing, dancing, and hugging! Branch is Poppy's best friend. He'll follow her on any adventure.

Poppy soon discovers that she and her friends are Pop Trolls— and they aren't the only Trolls in the world! There are all sorts of Trolls . . . like the Techno Trolls, led by King Trollex . . .

. . . and Country Western Trolls, like Hickory, who sing sad, sad songs out in the heartland of Lonesome Flats. Their rough-and-tumble leader, Delta Dawn, will do anything to protect her town from fancy outsiders, like . . .

. . . Barb and the Rocker Trolls. Queen Barb thinks only rock music ROCKS, and wants to make all the Trolls think the same. And she's got the rock army and guitar licks to make 'em!

Poppy plans to stand up to Barb. She believes that all the Trolls can find a way to harmonize, and she's determined to get them together to dance, hug, and sing as one!

Hickory wasn't doing anything to lift her mood, playing his guitar and singing a sad song about unrequited love. *Where do they get all these sad, sad songs?* Poppy thought.

Branch, on the other hand, thought the lyrics perfectly captured the way he was feeling. He wanted to be more than just Poppy's friend. Sighing, he lay back on the raft and stared up at the clouds in the sky.

Hickory came up next to Branch. "Something tells me your heart ain't in this mission."

"What do you mean?" Branch asked. "I'm here, aren't I?"

Hickory smiled. "Yeah, you're physically here. You're on the mission, all right. But your heart is with Miss Poppy."

Branch sat up, surprised that Hickory had guessed his secret so easily. "Hey, hold your horses!" Then he remembered Hickory's four-legged body. "I'm sorry. Is that offensive?"

Shaking his head, Hickory said, "Not as offensive as you thinking I can't see what's right in front of my eyes. Did you tell her yet?"

Branch looked down at the logs that formed the raft, picking at a splinter of wood. "I tried," he admitted. "But . . ." He whistled and made an explosion sound, letting Hickory know his attempt had bombed. "Look, if you need someone to build you a survival bunker, I'm your Troll. But talking about feelings? Not so much."

"I get it," Hickory said, laughing. "You two are pretty different."

"We are," Branch agreed.

"And if you *did* tell her, who knows if she'd even hear you," Hickory observed.

Branch frowned. "What do you mean by that?"

Hickory looked right into Branch's eyes, giving it to him straight. "Well, let's just say only one of you is doing the listening in this relationship. And it's not her." He paused for quite a while as Branch slowly swallowed this piece of information. Then, just to be absolutely clear, Hickory said, "It's you."

"Yeah, I got that, thanks," Branch said glumly.

"Uh, guys?" Poppy called to them from her position at the raft's steering wheel. "Look!"

Branch and Hickory looked at her. She was pointing at the sky. A giant spaceship was hovering over the river!

CHAPTER SEVENTEEN

"AAAAAH!" Branch screamed, popping into an action pose.

"What in buttered biscuits?" Hickory said.

"Wait," Poppy said, pulling out her map of the Trolls lands. The spaceship above them resembled an enormous chrome clam—just like the one pictured in Vibe City on the map. Colorful wavy stripes circled the top and the bottom. "I think we've found the Funk Trolls!" she said. But how were they going to get up there?

Waving her arms, Poppy tried to get the attention of the occupants of the huge spaceship. "Hey! Hey, down here!"

Her efforts worked. *FWOOOM!* A floodlight shot down from the ship.

"AAAAH!" Poppy screamed.

"Poppy!" Branch shouted.

A clear bubble formed around Poppy, lifting her up into the air.

"Well, how-dee—" Hickory started to say, amazed. But then a bubble formed around him. He tried fighting it off with his guitar, but it sucked him up into the air, too.

Branch couldn't believe what he was seeing. Then a bubble formed around him. He tried punching it, but it carried him off the raft, just like the others. The three bubbles floated straight up to the gigantic spaceship!

The bubbles arrived in a sleek, modern observation room with a big window. *POP!* Poppy's bubble burst. She dropped into a beanbag chair. *PLOP!*

POP! Hickory's bubble burst, and he was dropped into a beanbag chair right next to Poppy's. *PLOP!*

POP! Branch's bubble burst. But he missed his beanbag chair entirely, hitting the floor. *THUD!*

A voice said, "Welcome to Vibe City."

Poppy, Hickory, and Branch turned to see a Troll who looked just like Cooper, except he was wearing a gold-colored baseball cap over his dreadlocks, his neck had yellow stripes, and his chin sprouted a wispy beard. "You are hereby cordial guests of Prince Cooper," he announced politely.

"Cooper?" Poppy said, amazed. "What are you doing here?"

"You mean what am I doing over *here*?" Cooper said from the other side of the Trolls. When Poppy turned and saw her friend, she realized the Troll in the gold cap wasn't Cooper, even though he looked just like him. She kept turning her head from one Troll to the other, astonished to see two Coopers.

Branch was amazed, too. He tilted his head and smacked his ear as though there were water in it. "Okay," he said, "maybe all the jazz hasn't left my brain yet."

Laughing, Cooper took a step forward. "Oh, come on, Branch! It's me! Turns out I'm actually from Vibe City, just like my twin brother." He ran over and put an arm around the Troll with the gold cap. "Meet Prince D!"

"What's poppin'?" Prince D said, grinning. He and Cooper laughed and wrestled each other to the ground.

"I've got a twin brother!" Cooper said happily. He couldn't believe it!

Neither could Poppy. "How is this possible?" she asked.

Prince D stopped wrestling with Cooper. He stood up and explained. "When we were babies, Cooper's egg was carried off by a bird, and Mom and Dad could never find him. You guys raised him as one of your own." Prince D and Cooper laughed and put their arms around each other.

"So," Poppy said to Cooper, "that means you're a Funk Troll?"

Cooper shrugged. "You don't have to be just one thing. I'm Pop *and* Funk."

"Or maybe you're Hip-Hop," Prince D suggested. "Like me!"

"Hip-Hop?" Poppy asked. "Like Tiny Diamond?" Wondering how many Hip-Hop Trolls there were, she took the map of the Trolls lands out of her hair and inspected it closely, looking for a Hip-Hop Trolls land.

"Oh, Hip-Hop's not on your map," Prince D said, taking a look. "I think your map's a bit outdated."

"Hmmm . . . ," Poppy said, still studying it.

Branch took the map and looked at it. Then he looked at Poppy. "Oh, yeah, he's right. It still has Disco."

Two older Trolls entered the observation room. They resembled Cooper, but one was female and the other was male, and they both wore crowns and royal outfits. The male had a gold cape, a blue beard, gold goggles, and three toe rings. The female wore a beautiful white cloak with a gold-and-purple lining. Her silver headdress looked like fireworks.

Cooper smiled when he saw them. "Poppy," he said, "I want you to meet the King and Queen of Funk . . . my mom and dad."

Poppy gave a little curtsy.

"We want to thank you for taking care of our son for all these years," Queen Essence said.

"Wow, Cooper," Poppy said, "you look just like your dad."

"That must be why he's so good-looking," King Quincy said. "Ha, ha, ha!"

"Was that a dad joke?" Cooper said joyfully.

He ran to his parents and gave them a big hug. Prince D joined in, too, and they all wrapped their long necks around each other's necks. "Shower me with kisses!" Cooper said, and Queen Essence happily obliged. Then she and King Quincy walked over to Poppy, Branch, and Hickory.

"If there's anything we can do to repay you, anything at all, it would be our pleasure," King Quincy offered.

"Yes!" Poppy said gratefully. "We need your help in uniting the Trolls world to save all music from Queen Barb."

"All right," Queen Essence said. "What's your plan?"

"If we combine our music, she'll see that music unites all Trolls, and we're all the same, and that she's one of us," Poppy explained.

The Funk Trolls stood there a moment, not saying anything. It was an uncomfortable silence.

Finally, King Quincy spoke. "Poppy, I mean no disrespect, but King to Queen, anything but that."

"What?" Poppy said, taken aback. "Why not?"

King Quincy and Queen Essence exchanged a knowing look.

CHAPTER EIGHTEEN

To answer Poppy's question, the Funk Troll royal family led the Pop Trolls to Vibe City's Hall of Records. As they walked, Queen Essence said to her husband, "Now, Q, the Pop Trolls were good to our son."

"And for that I'm grateful," King Quincy acknowledged. "But it doesn't erase what they did to our music."

They entered the hall, which was full of shelves holding thousands of old-fashioned record albums. King Quincy pulled one off a shelf. It had a colorful cover that read HOW IT WENT DOWN." He opened it, then he turned to his son. "Let's tell 'em how it was, Prince D."

A beat started playing, and Prince D rapped a hip-hop song about the early history of Trolls music. It was very different from the history King Peppy had read in the Pop Trolls' ancient scroll.

In the early days, according to Prince D's lyrics, the Trolls from different tribes had gotten along. And even though the styles of music were unique, new sounds often came out of them playing their styles in tandem.

King Quincy pointed to a drawing on the album illustration that showed different colors coming together to form a magical instrument.

Prince D rapped that the Pop Trolls started making music so simple and catchy, it started to push the other styles of music out of the way.

The Funk King pointed to another picture. It showed a Pop Troll looking at colorful waves of music coming from a dark night sky.

Prince D then proclaimed that the strings had been separated to save all music from the Pop Trolls.

In the album's final illustration, the Trolls each took a string and ran. "The Trolls never lived in harmony again," King Quincy said sadly.

Poppy stared at the album in disbelief. Hickory

looked down at the ground, embarrassed for the Pop Trolls. Branch frowned.

"But this wasn't in our scrapbooks," Poppy said.

"Scrapbooks are cut, glued, and glittered by the winners," Prince D said.

Queen Essence spoke gently but firmly. "It may be hard for you to believe, but Pop Trolls tried to destroy our music."

"Just like Queen Barb is trying to do," Branch realized.

"As queen, I should have known," Poppy said. "But I can make it right."

"We can handle our own business, thank you very much," King Quincy said.

"But history is going to keep repeating itself until we make everyone realize that we're all the same," Poppy insisted.

King Quincy and Queen Essence made sour faces that showed they clearly disagreed. "But we're *not* all the same!" the king said.

"It's why all of our strings are different," Queen Essence said, stepping aside to reveal a bass guitar strung with one string—the Funk string. "Because they reflect our different music."

"Denying our differences is denying the truth of who we are," King Quincy said.

Poppy took all this in. "I hadn't thought of it like that," she admitted.

DOOWEET! DOOOWEEEET!

Sirens went off! The King and Queen looked alarmed. "Rock has arrived! It's on!" said Prince D.

King Quincy shouted, "Prepare for battle!"

"Oh, no!" Poppy cried.

"Assemble the crew!" Queen Essence commanded.

King Quincy turned to the gathered crew to give them his battle orders. Cooper took Poppy and Branch aside. "I'm going to make sure you get to safety," he assured them. He played a musical phrase on a keyboard, and two bubbles emerged, starting to surround Poppy, Branch, and Hickory.

But Poppy dodged the bubbles, trying to run deeper into the spaceship.

"Poppy!" Branch called. "What are you doing?"

"Not leaving!" she yelled back.

Branch ran after her, grabbed her arm, and pulled her into one of the bubbles with him. The bubble started to float out of Vibe City. "Poppy, we should go," he told her. "They said they don't want our help."

"No!" Poppy said, hammering against the bubble. "I want to make it better!"

"We've done enough," Branch said.

"No, Cooper!" Poppy protested.

"I love you, Poppy," Cooper said. "But I love them, too."

"No, no, no!" Poppy cried, banging her fists against the bubble.

Prince D handed Cooper a guitar to take into the musical battle with the Rocker Trolls. *FWOOMP!* The room was plunged into darkness.

"Rock cut the power!" Queen Essence shouted.

"They're fighting dirty," Prince D observed.

Poppy and Branch were shot out of the spaceship in one bubble, while Hickory was launched in another. The bubbles floated away from the ship.

"Hickory!" Poppy called to the Country Western Troll.

"Don't worry!" he called back. "I'll find you guys."

The bubbles floated off in different directions. Then Branch spotted the Rocker Trolls coming right at them. "Poppy!" he cried. Rock music blasted.

"Rock on!" Queen Barb called from her perch in one of the menacing fishlike Rocker vehicles. The spiny fish-creature pushed right past Poppy and Branch's bubble, jostling it as the Rockers headed for the Funk Trolls' spaceship. Queen Barb didn't even notice Poppy and Branch.

Poppy helplessly watched the Rocker Trolls go by. "Nooooo!" she howled.

CHAPTER NINETEEN

Poppy and Branch's bubble floated above the battle now raging between the Rocker Trolls and the Funk Trolls. The two Pop Trolls pressed against the side of their bubble, watching the mayhem below. Then Poppy turned to Branch in desperation.

"We have to get back down there!" she said. "I can't believe you wouldn't let me stay and help fight!"

"It's not our fight, Poppy," Branch said, sitting back against the bubble.

Poppy threw her hands up in frustration. "There's still hope! We could still fix this!"

Branch shook his head. "I've listened to you and

done it your way. Now it's *your* turn to listen. It's time to get back home."

"I'm not like you," Poppy said. "I can't just give up."

"Give up?" Branch said, hardly able to believe his ears. "I want to protect our friends and family!"

"I can't go home and face my dad now," Poppy said. "Not until I've proven myself as a good queen."

"So *that's* what this is really all about?" Branch said. "This whole thing has been about proving something to your dad?"

"Why are you so upset?"

"Because your dad was right," Branch said. "And Biggie was right. And Queen Essence was right. And I've been backing you up, even when you ignored them. But you never listen to me."

"Branch, what are you talking about?" Poppy asked, genuinely confused.

"You wanna be a good queen?" Branch asked. "Good queens actually listen. Know what I heard back there? Differences *do* matter. Like you and me. We're too different to get along. Just like all the other Trolls."

Poppy looked stunned.

POP! The bubble hit the ground and burst. Branch and Poppy tumbled out.

Standing and brushing off her dress, Poppy said, "We are really different."

Branch was hurt. He'd said they were different, but he didn't really want Poppy to agree with him. He wished she'd argue with him. He didn't tell her that, though. He just stood up and said, "So different."

Deep down, Poppy didn't really believe she and Branch were all that different. But when he'd said that she didn't listen, and that she wasn't a good queen, it had made her mad. She'd said they were different, so she was sticking with that, at least for now. "Completely out of harmony," Poppy said.

"Completely," Branch echoed. He couldn't think of anything else to say. He didn't like where the situation was going, but how could he stop it?

Poppy didn't know why Branch was acting so strange. She was confused. "I don't even know why we're friends," she blurted out.

"Neither do I," Branch said. He started to walk away. But then he turned back, and for a moment, he spoke from his heart. "So why do I care about you more than anybody else in the world? Weird, right?"

He sulked off into the woods, leaving Poppy alone, standing there with her mouth wide open.

Branch trudged through the forest, hoping to somehow find his way home. Inspired by Hickory's sad song, Branch began to make up his own mournful ballad about his love for Poppy. (Despite feeling terrible, he thought his song was pretty good.) As he sang, he imagined dancing with Poppy.

DING! His Hug Time bracelet went off, but there was no one to hug. He knelt by a creek, alone and heartbroken. For a moment, he sat in the clearing next to the burbling creek.

Then . . . music. K-Pop music.

In the forest?

To his surprise, a gang of K-Pop Trolls emerged from the trees and surrounded Branch, wrapping him up so he couldn't escape.

"Who are you guys?" he asked.

"We're the K-Pop Gang," their leader answered. "And we're taking you down, Pop Troll!"

"Uh, aren't we all Pop Trolls?" Branch asked, confused.

"No, we're *K*-Pop," the leader snarled. "It's completely different."

But before the K-Pop Trolls could do anything, another gang of Trolls emerged from the other side of the clearing: the Reggaeton Trolls.

"Reggaeton Trolls!" the K-Pop leader challenged. "You want him, you're gonna have to dance for him!"

"You're on!" answered the leader of the Reggaeton Trolls.

The two gangs of Trolls danced, showing off their best moves, trying to top each other. Branch joined them. In the end, both groups of Trolls were impressed.

"Respect," the K-Pop leader said.

"Respect!" the Reggaeton leader said, getting an idea. "Why don't we split him?" The K-Pop and Reggaeton Trolls loved it. They closed in on Branch.

"Wait, wait, wait, wait, wait," Branch stammered. "Why does Barb get to decide which music gets to be saved? *All* music should be saved."

The K-Pop Trolls and the Reggaeton Trolls

stared at Branch. *Is it working?* he thought. *Am I getting through to them?* He hadn't had much luck changing people's minds lately. . . .

They murmured in agreement. The Reggaeton leader, Tressillo, spoke. "All right, okay . . . I'm listening, Pop Troll."

Poppy sat on the ground, sad and alone. She pulled the pop string out of her hair and plucked it. *TWONNNG!* "Differences *do* matter," she said to herself.

RUSTLE, RUSTLE! She heard something moving in the woods behind her. Quickly hiding the string in her hair, she jumped to her feet, ready to face whatever emerged from the forest. From behind a big tree came . . . Hickory!

"Poppy!" he said, smiling. "There you are!"

"Hickory!" she said. "It's so good to see you!" She ran and gave him a big hug.

Hickory looked around. "Where's Branch?"

"We had a fight," Poppy admitted sadly. "He's gone. He's heading back to Trolls Village."

"That's a shame," Hickory said.

Poppy turned away. "I was so desperate to be a good queen that I stopped listening to anyone but myself. Including my best friend. It's all because of this stupid string." She reached up and pulled the pop string out of her hair. It glowed.

Hickory stared at the string. "Poppy, take your string and run as fast as you can! You hear me?"

"What are you talking about?" Poppy asked.

"Trust me," he pleaded. "Just go, please!"

Hickory's two back legs started moving around, stepping and kicking. His back end shook. He almost lost his balance. It was as if he'd lost control of the back half of his body. "Now please," he repeated, "just go!"

"Hickory, are you all right?" Poppy asked, concerned for her friend's health.

"I'm fine," Hickory said. He turned and spoke to his back end. "Hey, now! Stop that! Whoa, now! Hey! *Heeyah!*"

But his back half just kept moving—until a hand burst out of his side, feeling around like it was looking for something!

Horrified, Poppy watched as—*ZZZZZIP!*

CHAPTER TWENTY

The hand unzipped a hidden zipper, separating Hickory's back half from his front half. A short Troll with a big mustache stood behind Hickory, still wearing the back end of the Country Western Troll costume. His name was Dickory.

"Nein!" Dickory yelled at Hickory. "What are you doing?"

Poppy stared at the two Trolls. "What's going on, Hickory?"

"I'm so sorry," Hickory said.

"Yes, show her who you really are, Hickory," Dickory said, pulling down Hickory's costume to reveal a pair of lederhosen—the kind of short pants worn by yodel-ay-hee-hooing yodelers!

"*Yodel-ay-hee-hoo!*" Hickory yodeled.

"*Yodel-ay-hee—*" Dickory began in response.

"Wait," Poppy interrupted. "You're the Yodelers?"

"Ja, you're darn skippy, player play," Dickory confirmed.

"And you were gonna give our pop string to Queen Barb?" Poppy asked, feeling betrayed.

"Ding, ding!" Dickory said, touching his finger to his nose in the classic sign to say that she had guessed it correctly. "Give this person a strudel for the correct answer!"

"And you've been in back the whole time?" Poppy asked Dickory.

Dickory made a face. He clearly didn't want to discuss his time as the back half of a Country Western Troll. "Next subject, please."

Poppy was baffled. She looked at Hickory. "Why would you do this?"

"So sorry," he said, dropping his fake Country Western drawl and speaking in a completely different accent. "It was the only way to save our beautiful yodeling."

"Hickory . . . ," Dickory said, warning his fellow bounty hunter not to lose sight of their mission.

"But trust me," Hickory went on, "you need to get out of here right away."

"What are you doing, Hickory?" Dickory asked. Not waiting for an answer, the short Troll ran forward and grabbed the pop string. Poppy held on to it, and Hickory jumped in, trying to help Poppy. It was a three-way tug-of-war. Finally, Dickory managed to yank the string away from Poppy and Hickory. Waving it over his head, he yodeled triumphantly. *"YODEL-AY-HE-HOO!"*

Just then, Queen Barb stepped out of the shadows behind Hickory and Dickory.

"I thought I heard a yodel," she said, an evil smile spread across her face.

"Queen Barb!" Poppy said.

Barb glared at her rival with a triumphant twinkle in her eye. "Nice job, fellas," she told the bounty hunters. She snatched the string out of Dickory's hand and plucked it. *TWEEEENG!* A sweet pop tune rang out. "Final notes of pop." Barb was satisfied. "They'll never invade anyone's brain again."

"I'm not gonna let you do this!" Poppy said, full

of fierce determination.

But Barb just laughed, looking Poppy up and down. "This is who I've been worried about? This pipsqueak?"

Poppy looked defiant. "I'll *never* stop fighting until I make things right! And I'm *not* a pipsqueak!"

Walking right up to Poppy, Barb considered her height. "Uh, yeah you are. 'Cause I'm like a whole centimeter taller than you." She snapped her fingers. *SNAP!* Two of her Rocker Trolls appeared and hurried over to grab Poppy by her arms.

Poppy struggled to get free. "Leave me alone!"

"Leave me alone?" Barb repeated with sarcastic innocence. "I'm sorry, but *you* were the one who was all desperate to be best friends!"

Poppy kept trying to break loose of her captors. "Get your hands off me!"

"Ooh, okay, all right, you're a feisty one," Barb said. "I respect that. Strong woman to strong woman, am I right? You know who else was feisty? Trolls Village."

Poppy gasped. Barb and her Rocker Trolls must have already attacked her home! "Oh, no, no!" she cried, devastated as the Rocker Trolls carried her away.

Panting, Biggie had sprinted the last stretch to his beloved home village, carrying Mr. Dinkles in his arms. "Everyone! Everyone! We're ba-ack!"

But when he'd stepped into the clearing at the edge of the village, he was shocked to see that the entire village had been destroyed by Barb and her rock henchmen.

Half a dozen Pop Trolls crawled out of their hiding places to greet him.

"Biggie!" Guy Diamond called.

"Hello, Biggie," Legsly said.

"You won't believe it!" Guy Diamond said in his shimmering, auto-tuned voice. "We were attacked by Barb and her barbarians!"

Tiny Diamond peeked out of his father's hair. "She took everyone to Volcano Rock City! Ain't that right, Daddy?"

"That's right, Tiny Diamond," Guy said sadly.

Sucking his thumb, the little Troll jumped into his father's arms.

"Oh, no!" Biggie had cried, turning away, unable to bear the sight of the wrecked village. "I shouldn't have left Poppy! She wouldn't have left me! Never, no matter how scared she was!" He turned back to face his friends. "I've got to go help Poppy!"

"We're coming with you, Biggie!" Legsly said bravely. "We've gotta go save our best friend!"

Smidge looked doubtful. "But how?" she asked in her deep voice. "We'll never make it past Security!"

Tiny Diamond flexed the little muscle in his arm. "We'll overpower them with muscle!"

"Or with fashion!" Satin and Chenille said.

They flew into action, cutting fabric, sewing pieces together, and making perfect rock 'n' roll costumes to wear as disguises.

In her haste, Satin pricked her finger with a sewing needle. "Ouch!"

At the sight of a tiny drop of her blood, Biggie fainted and hit the ground. *FWOMP!*

CHAPTER TWENTY-ONE

Volcano Rock City was well named. A rocky volcano rose out of the sea, spewing smoke, ash, and lava. At the base of the volcano was a huge natural arena where the Rocker Trolls held their monstrously loud concerts.

Barb and King Thrash flew into Volcano Rock City atop one of their spiky fish, with Poppy trapped in the creature's mouth. Its long, sharp teeth were like the bars of a cage. "Rock 'n' roll!" the old king croaked as they approached their home island. Looking down, Queen Barb could see Rocker Trolls filing in for her big show. Her fingers played over imaginary solos, and her neck tingled

at the thought of head-banging. She couldn't wait
to ROCK!

Down in the arena, the Rocker Troll roadies were
unloading equipment. From a shadowy tunnel, the
Pop Trolls spied on them.

"Okay," Biggie whispered. "Let's go!" He led
the way as they crept toward the backstage area.

JINGLE-JANGLE! JINGLE-JANGLE!

The Rocker Troll roadies looked up when they
heard the jingling sound. They spotted the Pop
Trolls and yelled, "Hey, stop right there!"

The Pop Trolls froze. "Legsly," Biggie hissed. "I
told you not to wear your anklet!"

"But it's my thing!" Legsly protested.

The Rocker Troll stomped up to the Pop Trolls.
"Only Rocker Trolls are allowed backstage!" he
barked.

"Well," Biggie said, "we are genuine Hard
Rockers." They stepped out of the shadows,
revealing their costumes—slightly corny-looking
jumpsuits with shiny sequins. Biggie and Mr. Dinkles
both looked like Elvis Presley. They launched into a

bouncy early rock 'n' roll tune that was a pretty far cry from rock.

They finished, proud of their performance. The Rocker Troll's expression hadn't changed—he still had a snarl on his face. But he shrugged and said, "Okay, cool." He handed each of the disguised Pop Trolls an instrument. "Hurry up! The show's about to start, man! Queen Barb's about to go onstage! Let's do this!"

In another area backstage, Riff shoved Poppy into a cage. "I just want to say that you smell like bubble gum, and I'm very sorry," he apologized. He left, revealing Barb standing there, gloating.

"You're welcome," Barb said.

"For what?" Poppy asked. She couldn't imagine what she could possibly be grateful for. Barb had taken her string, thrown her in a barred cell, and destroyed her village.

"For making your dream come true," Barb explained, smiling a wicked smile. "Letting you hang out with me. Getting a little quality time with your new best friend."

"What?" Poppy exclaimed. "I'm not your best friend!"

"You don't have to be embarrassed," Barb said. "I get it. Being queen can be kind of lonely." She looked away from Poppy, lost in thought. "There's all this pressure to please your dad, and you're surrounded by people who say they're your friends but just tell you what you want to hear, and . . ." She looked back at Poppy. "You know, other than your terrible taste in clothing and music and general lifestyle, you and me are the same, Popsqueak."

"No," Poppy said firmly. "You and I are totally different."

Barb shook her head. "No. How I see it is we're just two queens who want to unite the Trolls Kingdom."

"You don't want to unite the Trolls world," Poppy said, gripping the bars. "You want to destroy it."

Looking annoyed, Barb said, "Nuh-uh! No way! Music has done nothing but divide us. And now that I have the final string, I can make us all One Nation of Trolls Under Rock."

"What are you going to do?" Poppy asked.

"Play the ultimate power chord, and then you'll see," Barb said as she picked up her guitar and attached the pop string. She gave it a long sniff.

Now united, the six strings glowed with a bright rainbow light. Barb turned to go out and greet the crowd. They roared as she appeared through a cloud of stage fog.

"Who wants to see what the ultimate power chord can do?" Barb roared. She spin her arm in a windmill, ready to strike the chord. She aimed her guitar at Poppy, and—*THUNK!*

A thick book fell from the sky and landed on Barb's head.

"I guess a giant comprehensive manual *does* come in handy," Branch said as he jumped down from Sheila B.'s basket.

"Branch!" Poppy cried out in joy.

Barb got to her feet, snarling. "Poppy's *boyfriend* came to crash the concert."

The Queen of the Rockers aimed the guitar at Poppy and played the chord. A mighty sound reverberated from the guitar—and Branch bravely leapt in front of Poppy.

Poppy held her breath and squeezed her eyes shut. When she opened them, Branch was standing before her as a long-haired Rocker Troll!

"ROCK ON!" he bellowed.

CHAPTER TWENTY-TWO

Queen Barb looked at the new Rocker Branch and grinned. "Oh, sick! It totally works!"

"You're turning everyone into Rock zombies?" Poppy said, appalled.

Barb gave a cheerful little nod. "Yep, and I can't wait to party with you."

Poppy crossed her arms across her chest. "You'll never turn me."

Barb began to play the guitar, aiming its power at the other Trolls. *No one was spared!* Even little Clampers yelled, "ROCK 'N' ROLL!"

All the Rocker Trolls cheered! The other kinds of Trolls lost their color as they became dark headbangers. One of them got so excited, he dove from his seat in the lower balcony, aiming for the mosh pit far below. "QUEEN BARB!" he shouted as he jumped. *SHPLORPSH!* He missed the mosh pit and landed bottom-first in a pool of bubbling hot lava. "YEOW!" He leapt away from the scorching liquid with the seat of his leather pants smoldering.

The band—Biggie and the other Pop Trolls—launched into a rock song. Barb rocked out on her guitar. Flame pots exploded, lighting up the faces of the Rocker Trolls in the audience. They oohed and aahed at the spectacle.

One Rocker Troll, moved by the sheer beauty of Barb's rocking performance, shed a single tear. The tear made the rocker sign with its fingers, shouting, "Rock on!"

As Barb played the six magical strings on her guitar, she shouted, "And now we're all going to live as one, and everyone is going to rock! Especially the Pop Trolls!"

While all this was going on, Poppy was busily picking the lock on her cell with her hair. As soon as the door swung open, she scrambled up the scaffolding.

"Not so fast, Popsqueak," Barb snarled. "Hey, boy toy, it's mullet time."

Branch's hair suddenly grew, but only in the back, creating a mullet hairdo. He lashed out with his new mullet and caught Poppy. He dragged her back to Barb, who cut loose with the full might of the power chord.

When the smoke cleared, Poppy stepped forward as a Rocker Troll! Barb nodded, and announced to the crowd, "Pop has become rock!"

Grinning, Barb tossed her guitar with the six magical strings to Poppy. She wanted the satisfaction of seeing the new Poppy transform all the other Trolls into Rocker Trolls. "Now finish them off!" she ordered.

Poppy started to play. Her fellow Pop Trolls looked horrified, but Poppy turned to the disguised band members and winked. The solo she was playing was definitely *not* Rock. It was bright, bouncy, and very catchy.

"Pop music?" Barb said, mystified and horrified. "What are you doing? You're supposed to be a rock zombie!" She couldn't understand why Poppy wasn't under her complete control, utterly transformed into a zombie of rock music and incapable of playing pop.

Smiling, Poppy pulled two gumdrops out of her ears. "Gumdrops!" she explained. "Soundproof and delicious!"

"Well, how-*dee*!" Hickory called from the audience, delighted that Poppy had learned his little trick for resisting the powers of hypnotic music.

"Give me that guitar!" Barb snarled, lunging at Poppy.

"No!" Poppy said. "You can't do this, Barb! I'm not going to get you do this to anyone else!"

Barb grabbed the neck of the guitar, but Poppy held on tight, refusing to let go. They struggled to gain control of the powerful instrument.

"A world where everyone looks the same and sounds the same?" Poppy said as they wrestled over the guitar. "That's not harmony!"

"Hey, Barb," Riff said, scratching his head as a new thought knocked around inside it. "If we all look the same, act the same, and dress the same, how will anyone know we're cool?"

"A good queen listens," Poppy explained. "Real harmony takes lots of voices. *Different voices!*"

Poppy raised the guitar high over her head with both hands and then slammed it down onto the stage. *SMASH!* The guitar shattered into pieces with the terrible sounds of squealing feedback. The six musical strings were destroyed!

CHAPTER TWENTY-THREE

With the strings destroyed, King Trollex, King Quincy, Queen Essence, Trollzart, Delta Dawn, and all the other Trolls turned back to their normal selves. Their eyes lit up, and color flowed back into their bodies and hair.

Branch returned to his old self, too. Poppy ran to him, calling his name in joy and relief. "Branch!"

Barb desperately tried to pick up what was left of the strings, but they crumbled to dust in her hands and slipped through her fingers, blowing away in the wind. "No!" she cried. "My strings! No!"

Furious, she turned to Poppy. "What have you done? You've destroyed music!" She turned to the crowd in the arena. "Give it up, everybody!" she shouted with raging sarcasm. "Thanks to the Pop Trolls queen, we've all lost our music! History repeats itself! Pop has ruined EVERYTHING!"

All the Trolls looked devastated—even Poppy, who fell to her knees and turned to the crowd, hoping for their forgiveness. How could they live without music? Everyone was silent.

But then . . . *THUMP-THUMP. THUMP-THUMP. THUMP-THUMP.*

A beat! A rhythm!

Cooper realized it was his heart beating. He held a microphone to his chest so everyone could hear it. Now amplified, his heartbeat sounded like a bass drum. *THUMP-THUMP. THUMP-THUMP. THUMP-THUMP.*

Cooper's twin brother, Prince D, started beatboxing over the sound of the heartbeat. "SH-THOOMPA DA BUH DOOM-DOOM BAH-DAH!"

Queen Essence smiled. "Those are my sons, making music!"

The Country Western Trolls started to stomp their feet in time to the rhythm, doing a line dance.

Poppy looked astonished. Queen Essence turned

to her and said, "Queen Barb can't take away something that is inside us. Because that's where music really comes from. Not from some string. Inside *all* of us."

The crowd gasped, amazed at what Queen Essence had said. Music without their strings? Was it possible? They started to nod in time to the music, smiling.

"It comes from our experiences . . . ," King Trollex said.

"Our lives . . . ," Delta Dawn added.

"Our culture . . . ," Queen Essence said.

Poppy slowly nodded, realizing the Funk queen was right. "Queen Barb can't take that away." She turned to the crowd, took a deep breath, and started to sing in time with the rhythms the other Trolls were making. *"Let me hear you sing!"*

Poppy's voice echoed through the huge arena. She turned to Branch, and they smiled at each other. She turned back to the audience and sang some more. Branch joined her, singing perfect harmony.

Barb couldn't believe this was happening. Music without the strings! "B-but . . . how?" she stammered. Did Poppy have a point? She turned to her father for guidance. "Dad?"

Sitting behind a keyboard, he said, finally speaking clearly, "It's all right, Barbara. Just let everyone be what they want to be. Including you."

One by one, the different tribes of Trolls joined Poppy's song. She and the Funk Trolls sang. Then the Country Western Trolls started playing each other's long tails like guitars with Poppy singing along.

The Techno Trolls sang in voices that sounded electronic. It was cold and mechanical, but at the same time, it was the perfect harmonic counterpoint to what the other Trolls were singing.

All the Trolls joined in—adding something special from deep inside themselves! The Funk Trolls clapped their hands. The Classical Trolls sang in big, operatic voices. The Rocker Trolls tapped out a rhythm with the spikes on their wristbands. Even Riff joined in the musical celebration, pounding out a steady beat!

"Let me hear you sing!" Poppy sang.

"Sing!" everyone answered.

Barb grabbed a guitar and started playing along. Her Mohawk grew taller and brighter. A rainbow wave spread through the crowd, making everyone lighter, brighter, and more colorful than ever before.

Trollzart waved his baton, leading the Classical Trolls. "Play!" he cried joyfully. "Play! Beautiful!"

"Sick!" Barb said happily as she played a sizzling guitar lick that complemented what the Classical Trolls had just added.

Everyone sang together.

Still playing her guitar, Barb crossed the stage to meet Poppy in the middle. The two of them sang together as new friends. When the song ended, Poppy and Barb were surrounded by their friends and the leaders of the all Trolls. Everyone cheered!

Poppy turned to Branch. "I love that we are so different."

"I love you, Queen Poppy!" he said. He had finally managed to tell Poppy how he felt about her!

"I love you, too, Branch," Poppy said, smiling.

"Shall we?" Branch suggested.

SMACK! High-fiving, they made a perfect connection!

CHAPTER TWENTY-FOUR

Working together, the Pop Trolls rebuilt their village in no time at all, making it even more colorful and fun than it had been before.

Poppy sat with a circle of young Trolls from all six tribes, showing them a new scrapbook she'd made. It told the history of the Trolls—the *true* history, which she'd learned on her adventure.

"In the beginning," she told the youngsters, "we were divided. Our ancestors thought we were just too different to get along."

Poppy turned the felt page to a picture of a wise old Troll.

"Turns out they were wrong," she said. "Very,

very wrong." She turned the page. Now the old Troll was slapping his head. In a speech balloon, he was saying, "We're sorry."

"You have to be able to listen to other voices, even when they don't agree with you," Poppy explained. "Our differences aren't bad. Our differences are good."

She turned the page again. The next two pages were full of flowers. They bloomed, and all the different kinds of Trolls—Funk, Classical, Techno, Pop, Country Western, and Rocker—popped out of the flowers, smiling.

"Our differences make us stronger," Poppy continued. "More creative. More inspired. So whether your song is sad and heartfelt, loud and defiant . . ."

She turned the page to show a picture of Delta Dawn strumming her guitar.

". . . or warm and funky . . ."

She turned that page, and there were King Quincy and Queen Essence, playing their funky music with their sons, Cooper and Prince D.

". . . you can't harmonize alone," she concluded, closing the scrapbook. Branch walked up to her, and she took his hand. They smiled. Then—*CHOMP!*

Clampers was biting the scrapbook with her big teeth!

"Clampers!" Poppy said. "Let's not eat our history!"

Clampers grinned an apologetic grin. "Sorry, Miss Poppy."

Tiny Diamond rode out on a toy dump truck. "Done with my nap and ready to play!" he announced, shooting glitter out of the truck.

Poppy laughed, and so did Branch.

And with that, the Trolls, from all parts of the kingdom, gathered together and partied through the night and into the next day, continuing for the rest of the week. The music never stopped!